Acknowledgements

To those that have known me in the past and have participated in making some of my own fantasies come to pass:

To Elise, for all the educational excursions at Volunteer State

To Dawn, for all the years at Middle Tennessee State

To Denise, for all the weekend trips to Garrett College

To Patrice, for all the nights after

Other books by Riley S. Brown:

The Chronicles of Ar Solon Series:

Book 18: Chains of Solace: (TBA)

Book 19: Forgotten Angel (Released April 2010)

Book 20: The Paths We All Walk: A Collection of Tales (TBA)

Book 21: The Healer (Released August 2011)

Book 21 ½: The Healer, Part II: (Fall 2014)

The Wunderlannd Series:

Edward in Wunderlannd (Released October 2011)

Edward and The Enfeebled (Released December 2012)

Writing under the alias Titus Strong:

A Man's Romance Novel Series:

The Temptress: Book One (Released August 2011)

A Corporate Feeling: Book Two (TBA)

Teach Me: Book Three (TBA)

How Santa Ate My Cookies and Other Festive Tales of

Erotic Fiction: Christmas Special (Released June 2014)

Available for purchase at:

www.barnesandnobles.com, www.amazon.com

The Temptress

BOOK ONE OF
A MAN'S ROMANCE NOVEL

BY

TITUS STRONG

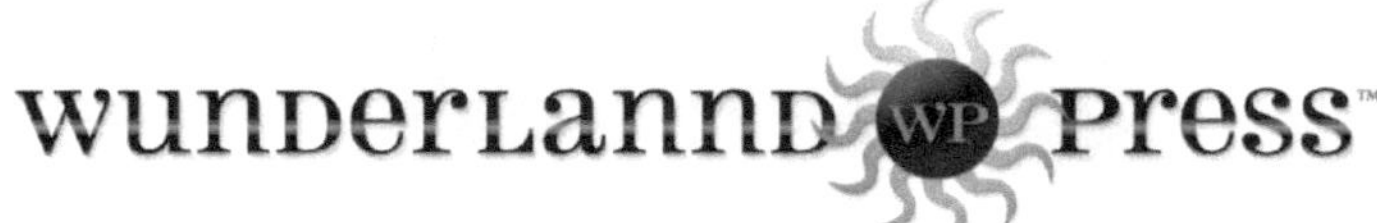

wunDerlannD WP press™

This is a work of fiction. Names, characters, places, and incidents are either the product of the author's imagination or are used fictitiously, and any resemblance to actual persons, living or dead, is entirely coincidental.

The Temptress:
Book One of a
Man's Romance Novel

Front and Back Cover Graphic Arts by Jen Street
Permission to be used and copyright © 2011
Copyright Year: 2011
Copyright Notice: by TITUS STRONG. All rights reserved.
The above information forms this copyright notice:
© 2011 by TITUS STRONG. All rights reserved.

Published by Wunderlannd Press Publishing
Baltimore, MD

This book, or parts thereof, may not be reproduced in any form without permission. For information, please contact the following at their email address: rileybrown90@hotmail.com

"Sex is dirty… if you do it right."

Isaac Asimov, from the novel,

The Sensuous Dirty Old Man

FOREWORD

<u>Every saga has a beginning...</u>

Too bad this isn't a saga. This is simply a series of novels that some guy, me, decided to put together for others, you. I started writing this series of books back in 1997. Yeah, a long fucking time ago, in a state far, far away from where I am now. I was pent up and sexually frustrated to say the least. I had gone through quite an operation and it had messed up my man parts something fierce at an early age.

In those few months that I wasn't able to use them, I created this character and these storylines, hoping to get out what I couldn't onto the page, (don't take that out of context) and create a sort of punching bag for my sexual feelings. I was going through a divorce and was hating on some women in my life, so I vented.

And here is the final product... 14 years later, in print, sitting on a shelf or on a table being sold. I never thought this was entertainment enough for those out there, so I only gave copies out to a select few to read. However, as I was finishing up on another novel, I blew the dust off of this one and started to let others read it again. This was in 2010 and the responses that I got back were great. The readers stated that it was funny, that they couldn't wait for the follow-up to the story, and it was just plain fun for them. Well, I had to pursue the compliments to another level.

But, with a cover like this and a catchy title, this is the last shit you want to hear, so I'll get to the good stuff...now.

<u>A little advice...</u>

Say that you spend most of your life with one person or a small number of people (5 or less) and you keep your fantasies and dreams about intimacy a secret from those that you're with. Let's say that you do that. Then what happens? Have you become what your potential allows you or have you limited yourself?

The only reason that I ask this is that this is what this book series is about; limits. Do you have limits, standards, ethics and morals about intimacy? If you do, some of this book will offend you. If you're riding the line (*sad if you are*), then you might love this book series. If you play it safe in regards to sex play and intimacy, then this will be your new addiction.

This is not an explanation or an apology as to why this book is written the way it is. In fact, this is the opposite of that. If you picked up this book, you know by now that you did not use your better judgment as you normally would and invest your money and time in something truly fulfilling.

This is a smut book.

The cover denotes that this is explicit and the journey of the two main characters, Mark and Denise Malone is just that.

I must admit that I was a little bit hesitant in regards to releasing this novel series due to its content until I realized that we are all perverts inside. Somewhere, whether it's on the surface of ourselves or deep within the parts where we limit ourselves oh so much, there is a perverted man/woman waiting to get out and lay waste to others by putting them in compromising sexual situations and pushing the limits.

This novel pushes the limits. The next two in this series will do beyond what this first book of the series set out to do. Prepare yourself. Enjoy tiptoeing through this naughty delight.

Go do something naughty in your own life after reading this so you can feel less awkward with the fact that fictional characters in this book are having more fun than you.

Go fuck someone!

Titus Strong

In a compromising position

July 9, 2011

Chapter One

- "A BIRD IN THE HAND..." -

"Bring me my wine, will you darling?" She spoke and, when she did, he listened. In fact, everyone seemed to listen to her. She was a beautiful, rich, charming and magnificent piece of work. Several times, lying in bed next to her he would just stare at her, wondering what kind of god could make something so beautiful. She was dazzling. Every man she had ever met, and even some she hadn't, wanted her, had dreams about her, even stalked her.

However, her husband felt different than everyone else did. He knew behind all that make-up, fancy clothes, expensive jewelry and rich fragrances was just a scared, insecure young woman that he had met in college all those years ago. He looked at her now, in her silk blouse and matching miniskirt, sitting on the patio outside their home. They owned two other homes, also. The first he had bought with his money from his first big art showing. Then, when Denise began to get a little more famous in the film industry, she bought this one in Beverly Hills and another in New York; a thick, smoky, naughty little condo, decorated dark black and bright white, a very contrast place that Mark never really liked.

She had changed when she became a star, he thought, bringing her a glass of wine along with the rest of the bottle. He placed the glass in her hand as she spoke to her agent, yelling at the cell phone as if it affected the outcome of what happened in the next few moments after. Actually, it might have.

"Listen, I'm not taking the part unless they give me 7 million. That's my final offer! Dammit, Gene! You promised me this part! You better get it!" There was a pause and then she continued.

"I don't care about that other bimbo, Clarisse, or whatever her name is. She can just kiss my ass! Does she have any experience? My god, Gene, if I get out staged by a little whore who gives it up every time for a part in a movie you can just find a new client, you hear?" She dropped the call and sat the cell phone down on the table nearby, drinking from the glass. She gulped it down and reached for the bottle, pouring herself another. She must have seen the look on her husband's face or she wouldn't have said anything.

"What? I told him I'm not going to take anything less. He's just going to have to make other arrangements to settle with them, kiss their asses for awhile or find another job." Her husband wasn't surprised; not in the least. This was the third agent she had and he had almost quit twice last month.

Yes, her husband thought, *there would be a fourth Mr. Leech feasting on the nest egg before the month's over.*

Mark smiled his regular agreeable smile so as not to get her angry, which was really hard to do nowadays, and walked back into the house, hands in his pockets.

Yes, she had changed a lot since they met. She never used to drink. And, when she did finally start, it was always just us and no one else in our life. That's how Mark had liked it.

Now, there were cameramen outside snapping everything they could get close to. Shit, they can't even walk outside to get their paper. Mark looked down the hill to where the camera crews parked just outside the gate.

Yes, they were in for something, they knew all right. Once she drank too much, Denise got out of hand. After seven o'clock, the hired help left and it was just her and Mark. Sometimes Mark regretted marrying her just for the sheer fact that she had transformed, literally overnight, into a cruel bitch. But the sex was great, except for the fact that it wasn't with his wife. Sure, the first time he had cheated on her he had felt a twinge of guilt. But, after that, he began to get an exhilarating feeling from each affair he had.

*   *   *

It had all started with his masseuse, a sweet, twenty-one-year-old blond with a to-die-for body. She had been a replacement for a week while his other masseuse went on vacation. Sure, she was expensive, but money wasn't really anything to Mark since his wife had millions in the bank.

The masseuse was sweet, shy about sex when it entered the conversations they had but, when it came to her touch, her fingers and hands could stroke places on his body that would bring his senses jolting in pleasure. Mark's wife was out of town one week when his masseuse came for the weekly visit. And, while she was giving him and oil rub down that day, Mark got aroused. She couldn't help but look down at the towel that was standing up because of her. Mark was a little shocked also because his other masseuse, Olga, hadn't done that to him.

But Missy, his new masseuse, offered a sight that was as tempting as a fresh apple that hung only inches from his reach. He had to try and pluck it. He knew he would regret it if he didn't. Mark reached out and grabbed Missy's hand, rubbing her slippery palm across his chest and down under the towel to what had captured her attention. When her small fingers wrapped around it,

Mark could tell by the look in her eyes that she wanted him. She smiled.

And it wasn't a hello greeting smile or a "nice to see you" smile. Mark's cock was in her hand and she was smiling back, in full agreement at what Mark had planned for her and his oiled-down body. Her hand began stroking it; slow at first, and then soon she was tugging at his fullness, waiting for him to explode into her waiting hands. But he held back, waiting for her to give in. She did. Her blond head was down in between the folds of the towel in no time, lips wrapping about his manhood, Missy's short fingernails digging into his thighs.

Mark lie back down on the massage bed and let her devour him whole in her mouth, Missy slowly stripping off her clothes. This young masseuse had stirred something within him. He could feel the orgasm pulse in his body and he had to get her to stop soon. He grabbed her head and lifted it up. Missy's eyes, glazed over, her chest rising and falling with each new breath she took, was waiting for his next move. Mark knew what she needed.

He helped her off with the rest of her clothes, her tender, tanned breasts popping out of the bra she wore under her work clothes. He pressed one of her breasts into his mouth immediately. She pulled him closer, turning to the massage bed, one leg on it as Mark led her the rest of the way up. Missy was laying on the massage bed now, Mark moving in between her legs, mouth suckling on her breasts, a reassuring moan out of Missy's taunting lips telling him that his technique was effective.

He reached down between her legs, his fingers peeling the wet panties off, dropping them to the floor. He pressed two fingers into her moistness, probing for a tender spot. Her eyes closed and soon she began to move where his fingers moved, following tips of them, feeling them stroke the inside of her. This turned Mark on, too. He knew that it was time to move in, whether she could handle it or not.

Missy definitely wanted him to. As soon as he entered her, she moaned in pleasure, wrapping her arms around his neck. He plunged in deeper, feeling the insides of her tugging at him, his cock pressing deeper inside, waiting for her orgasm. She was almost there, he could tell. She began calling out his name.

"Oh my god, Mr. Malone! That feels so good. Please go faster! I want to feel it when you come inside of me. I like men who can come hard. Can you come hard, Mr. Malone?" She looked up at him just about as he was about come. She began to climax when he began to speed up. Her eyes closed tightly, she followed his rhythm, legs wrapped around his thighs which were now dripping with sweat and still slippery from the body oils. Mark looked down at her.

The power of her orgasm caught her off guard. She screamed out in pleasure, wrapping her legs tighter around her client, soaking him with her juices as she succumbed to each and every one of his thrusts. He slowed down for a moment, letting her catch her breath.

"How do you like that, Missy? Is that good enough for you?"

"God, that felt good Mr. Malone! Do you have any other surprises for me today?" Mark was still aroused after his orgasm. He could go for hours at a time but knew that this little flower of a woman couldn't stand it.

He pressed the matter though.

How much could she take? Mark slid her thighs back over onto the massage table and began kissing her neck, tonguing off the oils and sweat. He whispered in her ear.

"Missy, do you like orgasms? Do they make you feel good?" Mark, before she had a chance to answer, flipped her over onto her stomach, pushing himself back into her from behind. She was sweaty now, still panting from her first orgasm. She turned her head around to see Mark.

"I like it this way the most, Mr. Malone. Will you hold my breasts while you take me from behind?" Mark knew what she was doing. These were always his favorite kind of games. He loved for women to talk dirty to him. His wife hadn't done that in years.

He grabbed Missy's breasts and began drumming her from behind, feeling another orgasm pulse through his insides, soon coming out all over Missy's firm, round ass. She loved it all.

They went after each other again that afternoon, each taking turns being in control, fucking the other as hard as they could. Soon, the Mr. Malone was gone from her voice, replaced by Mark, her love god.

"Mark, fuck me! Fuck me like you fuck your wife!" Mark suppressed the smirk as much as he could.

If he did that, he thought, *she would fall asleep*. This was the first time sex had been fun for him in years. He had taken a little flower and left her dripping wet and out of breath. He was getting older, he knew, but he still had the sex drive that he had when he was younger.

*   *   *

Missy was the first in his line of affairs. It was something for him to strive at, to challenge him physically.

Mark had to find other ways to have fun. He began to travel, taking little excursions to the tourist states while his wife was working on a new movie in Paris. But she didn't mind. Actually, she liked him to be out of her way while she made her appearances and he really didn't mind at all.

The first state was New York. He made his way through the small Syracuse airport, dodging foreigners and runaway children, making his way to the baggage claim to collect his bags. When he got there, there was at least half the population of the airport waiting, pushing and shoving to grab their miscellaneous items, shouting obscenities, almost getting into a brawl to grab their valuables.

Mark just stood back watching, the crowd far from dying down. While he stood there, his mind wandered, filled with excitement that he was finally getting out of the house for a change. *I've been cooped up there too long*, Mark thought, spinning around the places in his mind he could travel to while he was out.

He had completely missed the woman standing next to him until she tapped him on the shoulder. He turned. To his immediate left, her smile dropping him to one knee, was a beauty. She was a slim, tall redheaded enchantress. Her body was sleek, like a supermodels', petite and curvy. She wore a pair of Ray-ban sunglasses that covered her eyes, the Calvin Klein T-shirt loose and hanging off one shoulder, a pair of cut-off jeans hugging her ass, showing more thigh than they were supposed to. Her voice was soft and calm.

"Pretty pitiful, huh? I'd hate to get in their way. You might come back missing a couple of fingers." Mark had to smile. He let out a little chuckle, just to keep her talking. She held out her hand. He took it.

"Cassandra Leonard. I'm a photographer from Oregon. And you are..." She noticed him staring at her. Mark tried to collect his thoughts the best he could, spitting out his name as if it were a bad taste in his mouth.

"Mark Malone. I'm a freelance artist. I paint art for different people, mostly rich assholes who have too much money." She nodded her head in approval. He must have passed her first test.

You stupid fuck, he thought to himself. *Relax, just relax. She is awesome, I know. Just concentrate on the here and now. Then the other things will fall into place.*

"So, where are you off to, Mrs. Leonard? Taking pictures of the stars for the Grammies this month or what?" She took off her ray-bans.

My god, she's perfect. Her green eyes stared out at him. He felt his blood begin to boil. He looked over at the baggage claim. The entire crowd was gone now, only a few parcels and suitcases circling aimlessly around on the track like a carousel. His bag circled twice.

Fuck it. I'll get it later. He waited for her answer.

"It's Ms., and no. I'm taking pictures at the Syracuse game tomorrow for the paper I work for. There are a lot of fans of Syracuse in Oregon, I have no idea why."

Did she just say Ms.? This must be a calling. This has to be happening for a reason.

Mark was always skeptical about the word *calling* or *karma* and all the other gypsy weirdo words, but something was buzzing around his head at the moment and, for some reason, it was that word.

Calling. He **had** to pursue. Mark went to retrieve his bag, catching up to it before it went around a third time. He returned back to Cassandra. She was writing something down on a piece of paper. She handed it to him.

"This is the hotel I'm going to be staying at for the next couple of days while I'm here. Call if you're in the Syracuse area and would like to see the game. I can get you some tickets. Do you like football?" He couldn't act stupid. He looked at the number and slid it into his khaki shorts pocket, lifting the suitcase strap up onto his shoulder.

"No, not really. But maybe if you want to get together after the game we could go out. You know, back to my hotel." He looked down at his left ring finger, checking.

Good, he forgot to put it on before he left. It must still be sitting on the bedside table, where it always sat.

He was safe. He waited for a reply. She was smiling.

I guess that was her answer. Cassandra saw her bag pass on the conveyer belt and stepped around Mark, her sweet smelling fragrance lingering for moments longer.

"Oh, look, there's my bag. Well, okay then. Call me around twelve or so. I have to take some after-the-game shots but I'll be back by then. Until then?" She reached out her hand. He took it, keeping a grip on it a moment longer.

Yes, there was something about her. He let Cassandra claim her bags, smelling her fragrance on him as he walked out through the sliding glass doors. Mark spotted his limo and driver moments later, his driver steadfast and ready. The driver grabbed his bags immediately and placed them in the trunk, closing the door behind Mr. Malone.

The limo drove off.

Chapter Two

- "MAY I TAKE YOUR ORDER?" -

The first place he went to was to the nearest shopping center. He hadn't been to one in a while and wanted to see what kind of things had changed in the past two years since he had been cooped up in his home. Most of his clothes he had on now came from some expensive shop in a row of glamorous stores that his wife took him to, flaunting him in front of the newspaper and video cameras everywhere she went while she was in town.

But most didn't know of me at all, or not at this mall, anyway. Sure, a couple of people stared at him as if he was an old friend, trying to place a name to his face. But he disregarded them and kept to his shopping, buying whatever appealed to him. Shirts, ties, a few nice pairs of shoes, whatever was on his mind or if he passed a shop that he liked, he would go in and look, most of the time leaving with a bagful of goodies.

Soon, the limo driver had to put up the first load of boxes and bags, returning with empty hands for more. Mark had fun for the first time in years, shopping without hundreds around him. Presently, he had began to hate the path his life had taken, seeing it as empty and with no purpose, letting his wife lead him around like a lost little puppy to her movie premiers.

But now, Mark had a different outlook on things. Of course, just one outing didn't change his perspective on life or anything, but it did make him feel a little bit better to see something besides the paparazzi and his wife's face and matching bitchy attitude.

He had agreed most of the way here on the plane that he did spend too much time at home, vegging out on the sofa, letting the t.v. think for him. And his diet of chips, salsa, and carbonated beverages did a number on his energy levels, too. He had stopped painting, stopped taking clients except when they harassed him too much, and he had tired of going out all the time to parties with his wife's friends. He hated to say this, but he didn't even have friends of his own anymore.

Mark handed a few more bags to his driver, stuffing the bags in one another so the driver could carry the load he had already acquired in just a few shops. The old chauffeur was quiet today. He had a somber expression on his face and didn't say much throughout the day.

Mark's thoughts went back to his life again. He had almost had enough of filling his life with material things such as new cars and boats, and houses. He wanted experiences and new happenings; things that he always wanted to do but never did. But it wasn't like he didn't like spending money. And Denise didn't mind him spending money. He could do whatever he wanted, really. He had just started feeling good when he and Missy had started and now he was here, looking for another piece of inspiration.

Sure, guilt was a factor. But it's a factor for everything.

Like the dollar on the ground or eating the last slice of pizza in a crowded room, or stinking up the bathroom.

But you have to learn to deal with each piece of guilt at a time and differently for that matter. This is how he handled guilt.

Avoid it, cause more guilty situations.

It looked like a vicious cycle, but only so much could be done in one day then it's over, just like the next and the next after that. This made him feel great. Now there was some excitement in his life.

And, for a fact, excitement is needed in everyone's life, whether they wanted it or not. Mark was sure he had read that somewhere in one of his wife's Cosmos.

Hours and hours went by on Mark's watch, the hands turning finally to six.

It was six o'clock and all was well, Mark watching the sun sink into the city landscape, the glass windows tinting over so he could stare at the sun as it sank into the buildings miles away.

I need to do this more often.

After a little while, Mark got tired of shopping and let his driver go for a time, watching as the old man left with the last of his bags.

Truthfully, Mark thought, *for an old man, he sure could keep up.*

Mark made his way to the food center. It seemed like the center was miles long, with at least two or three dozen different places to eat. He missed this also. A greasy cheeseburger and matching fries beat the dinners he and his wife went to any day.

Mark finally found a short line and jumped on the tail end of it, looking up at the sign.

The Golden Arch.

He ordered something and planted down at the nearest table, taking bite after delicious bite. He looked around at the signs, listened to the music played on the speakers hanging from every which way, followed asses as they danced around the mall "stage".

That's all this was, really; a stage for something to happen. A meeting place of sorts.

He chewed on another bite and pondered a little deeper.

That's all it was really. Just a different setting, a different time, the same things happening. Every day we fill with our lives with distractions, workdays, vacation time, movies, books, and a task of epic proportions just so we say that we have a life. But everybody has a life; it's just rated on an excitement scale of 1-10.

Mark scanned the mall, his rating scale popping up numbers in his head.

She's definitely a 7. Looks like she's got a lot on her mind. And him, he's definitely a 2. The janitor caught Mark staring at him and Mark smiled him off and went to another.

It was tricky. Could be a 5 or a 6, no way any lower. Not with a body like that. He stared at her.

She was tall, about an inch or two shorter than him, with brownish blond hair that came down to her shoulders. She was just a teen, probably eighteen or so. She worked at the Golden Arch, at the counter, taking orders. She hadn't taken his order though. He looked at her longer, waiting for a reaction. Soon, as if she could feel someone staring at her, she looked around. She found him staring at her. She smiled.

Definitely a 7.

Usually young girls turn away from an older man's gaze, but this one didn't. Mark got up and threw his trash away, returning his tray to the Golden Arch. He gave her the tray. She lingered near him, waiting for something. He reached out and took hold of her arm lightly, moving her closer. The customers watched, their gazes like the cameramen that followed Denise around. Mark looked back at her, glancing quickly at her nametag before whispering in her ear.

"Hey....Stephanie, what time do you get off?" Stephanie looked up into his gaze. She spoke.

"Why do you want to know?" He could tell that she was a little upset that he still held her arm so he let his grip loosen, his hand trailing down her arm. He could feel her fingers rub against the inside of his hand as he pulled away.

Definitely a signal.

"What would you say to a little ride in my limo?" Mark knew this sounded crazy but he didn't want to play games.

This was a workplace, not a chat line.

"I get off in fifteen minutes. Why?"

Mark leaned over the counter, closer to her. He had to take the chance. He didn't want to risk feeling like a dirty old man but it had to be done.

"It looks like you use a break from the norm. My limo's right outside. How does that sound?"

She could hear the desperation in his voice. It had been two months since his last encounter with Missy and he had masturbated several times after that, not being able to wait for his wife to return from her movie shoot. Stephanie smiled even wider when she heard that want in his voice. She leaned against the counter, her shirt hanging open a little for his viewing pleasure.

"I have my own ride."

"I can guarantee you don't have anything like I could give you."

"That can be argued. How about a maybe?"

"I'll be outside fifteen minutes after your shift ends."

She nodded and returned back to work, letting Mark walk out to his limo.

He wondered if she was going to show. She was probably in a relationship of some sorts with some young guy but he didn't care. All he wanted was something to tide him over until tomorrow night when he met up with Cassandra.

A new limo driver was waiting for him, an older man with a neatly trimmed gray moustache and matching hairpiece. Mark suggested keeping his hat on while outside the limo. The old man nodded.

Mark reached into his pocket and pulled out a hundred dollar bill, slipping it into the chauffeur's hand. The old man looked down.

"This is for a tight-lipped limo driver. Are you a tight-lipped limo driver?"

The chauffeur nodded while closing the door, pretending to zip his lips up. Mark smiled and leaned back into the plush leather seats.   It was about twenty minutes later when Stephanie approached the limo, the chauffeur opening the door, his arm pointing down and into the limo. She leaned her head in and looked at Mark, putting one foot in and then the other. She laid her purse down in the seat opposite to Mark and moved past him, sitting down. The driver shut the door and got into the driver's seat.

He looked over at Stephanie, who was looking around the limo, her eyes resting on Mark after a moment of getting her bearings. Her hand reached out to Mark, sliding down his leg, stopping at the zipper on his pants.

"No, I want to start slow. And I want to start first. Okay?" She nodded, not knowing what to say. Mark hit the intercom button to speak to the chauffeur. The chauffeur answered.

"Yes, sir. Can I be of service?" Mark smiled. He had a plan of where to go and how long it would take. He was getting good at this.

"Yes. Could you start towards Rochester and I'll tell you when to stop, okay?" The chauffeur comprehended by simply nodding his head.

He knew what was about to happen in the backseat. Hell, he probably wished he could be back here, too. The chauffeur began to drive, the black limo pulling slowly away from the mall parking lot and to the interstate.

Mark got back to Stephanie, who was already removing her work shirt, her breasts nearly bursting out of her bra. She had much larger breasts than Missy, his hands grasping them and slipping them out of her bra. They fell into his hands, his pants already beginning to bulge. He pressed her nipples in between his fingers and bit on them a little, feeling as they hardened inside his mouth.

He wanted this little cherry bad.

How would it feel to bang a teen in a limo?

He had fucked girls in college in his car in the backseat when his roommate wouldn't leave the dorm, but with the limo moving and the landscape skimming past, it brought a whole new sense of pleasure to the idea.

The question lingered on his mind as Mark sucked on her nipples, rubbing between her legs while she slowly unzipped her pants. She wore some light blue panties dotted with little red and yellow flowers.

They came off with a flick of Mark's wrist.

She was nervous, he could tell, but as her heart began to beat faster, Stephanie's senses became attuned to what was about to happen. Mark moved his head down between her legs, his tongue going to work immediately, rubbing at the insides of her.

She moaned lightly and started to slide down into the seat. He pushed her back up; keeping her up, pressing his tongue against her clit. She started moaning and writhing more, running her fingers through his hair, clawing at the back of his neck. Mark stayed in between her legs, tonguing her wetness until she bolted upright, squeezing his head between her legs. She came fast.

"Oh fuck, oh fuck, oh fuck!" Her legs tightened around him even more, her fingers holding his head in place until the orgasm subsided.

"That felt soooo good!" He moved away then, sitting in the seat opposite to her. He could see from the dim lights in the limo that she had already come hard but she wanted more than just a tongue inside of her.

It was time to see what she would do. He waited.

She moved over to him, her fingers loosening his belt, quickly unzipping his pants to get to his cock. Stephanie pulled it out, accepting it eagerly into her mouth. She worked on it fast, the best blowjob Mark had in a long time.

She pressed Mark's cock deep into her throat, almost gagging herself, taking it all in as if she were a professional at it. Mark leaned back against the plush leather of the limo, feeling

Stephanie's teeth slide up and down against his shaft, just enough to keep him on the edge of climaxing, watching her head nod up and down rhythmically. His hand reached for her hair and kept her going, faster and faster, his orgasm approaching.

"I'm getting ready to come." She slowed, pulling her mouth from its tight grasp on his cock and looked up at him, her hand now sliding up and down his shaft. He felt his load coming. It burst out into the open, her mouth on the tip of his penis just as he erupted. She swallowed all of his cum, squeezing on his thighs as Mark let out a stiff moan.

He barely had time to finish when she approached him from another angle. Stephanie grabbed onto his shirt, unbuttoning it as she climbed closer. The shirt was unbuttoned in no time and she slid it off, sliding down onto his lap as she did so. With one hand she grabbed his cock and with the other she gripped his shoulder, sinking her nails into his skin. Mark slid into her easily.

"God, mister, you have a big cock!" He grabbed her breasts and began to tease them with his tongue, touching them just enough to get a reaction out of her. She began to ride him, not really knowing how, Mark could tell, but trying her best. Her rhythm was off so he steadied her with his hands, holding her hips, pushing himself into her, inch by inch.

"You feel so good inside of me!" She let the words push out of her with every thrust, every slow plunge making her eyes close in pleasure. Mark could feel the beginnings of another orgasm inside of him so he leaned up to her and laid her on her back on the seats in front of him, lifting her legs up over his shoulders.

God, this felt good! These young girls were educated compared to when he had started dating. If he had even attempted something like this back in the day he would've got a flat rejection.

He looked down at Stephanie. Her eyes were closed and her mouth was open just enough to let out little moans of pleasure. She was wet but still tight inside and she raked at his back, her legs shaking from each thrust.

"Does that feel good, Steph? Does it feel good to give a customer what he wants?" She replied with an orgasm, her legs stiffening up on him, her tightness pulling at him, making him weak.

He could feel the orgasm starting to build up again inside of him. Stephanie stopped after the orgasm, out of breath, soaked with her own juices. She looked up at him. He was about to burst. Mark pulled his cock out and started masturbating, feeling the pressure of his load build up even more.

Stephanie moved her legs down off of his shoulders, waiting, her face near the head of his cock, her hands steadying him. She brushed his hand away when he started moaning and she continued for him, her mouth on the tip now, rubbing it with the roof of her mouth.

He came.

She kept him in her mouth, her hands moving over the length of his cock, filling her mouth with his pleasure, a little remainder dripping out onto her lips. She licked it off.

This girl was good.

Mark sat down next to her, looking at her wet, sex-drenched body and watched as she began putting her clothes back on. Mark followed her lead and slipped his own pants on.

"You were really good, Stephanie. You mind if I ask you a personal question?" She fastened her bra and slipped her shirt on, buttoning it up.

"Sure, as long as I can ask questions, too." He nodded.

"Mine first. How did you learn to suck a cock like that? Do they give classes now?" Stephanie laughed, her youth coming out in each giggle.

She really was quite attractive. Her face was flushed and the curve of it was perfect. She stopped laughing a moment later and answered.

"I used to have a boyfriend who liked for me to give him oral all the time. He didn't really like sex with me, though. Then, a few months later, I found out that he was gay. Apparently, he was trying the "straight thing" one more time before he gave up completely. That tripped me out. Since then, I've sort of stopped dating. No other reason than that, really." She paused, slipping her shoes on.

"Okay, it's my turn. Why did you pick me up? You're really an attractive guy. I'm sure you can get anybody you want." She grabbed her purse, sorting through it, pulling out her make-up. She fixed on her lipstick and blush.

"I picked you because you have a nice smile and beautiful tits; but also because there were no hassles with you. I just asked and you gave me an answer. I like that in a woman."

Mark didn't want to make this an odd situation, but he had to ask.

"Do you have anything to do the rest of the night? I have a lot more where that came from."

Sadly, Stephanie declined.

"Actually, I work the morning shift as well. I don't get any breaks here. I'm constantly working."

Mark clicked the intercom button and informed the driver to take them back to the mall.

Stephanie looked into her little mirror, straightening her hair. Mark almost wished that he were younger. He liked hanging out with younger women for some reason now. She was quiet most of the ride back. When they arrived at the mall where her car was parked, the chauffeur got out and opened the door, letting her out. She turned back to Mark, a questioning look on her face.

"By the way, what's your name?"

"It's Mark. Why do you ask?"

"You were an excellent fuck, Mark. Just wanted to let you know. And you know where I work. Come by anytime."

As the limo pulled away from the empty mall parking lot, the intercom clicked on, and the driver's voice piped up.

"Sir, may I suggest something next time?" Mark answered.

"Yes, what is it you'd like to suggest? I know she was young but she was good. Is that what this is about?"

"Yes sir, in a way. Sir, the next time a thing like this happens just remember to turn off the intercom before you start. You almost made me run off the road."

Mark fell over with laughter.

Chapter Three

- LAID AND PAID -

Mark woke that morning in his suite, the sun glaring menacingly at him through the window blinds. He rolled out of bed, clicking on the bedside lamp, walking over to the blinds. Mark closed them completely and walked back over to the lamp, sifting through the dresser drawer, which held everything in his pockets plus all his jewelry that he wore from the night before. He found Cassandra's number and slid it into his wallet, throwing it back into the drawer, looking over at the clock.

Eleven already? Shit! Most of the day's gone! He made his way into the shower. Soon, Mark was leaning against the shower wall, the hot water running on his back, slowly waking him up.

He remembered last night with Stephanie. He really would have to get in contact with her again.

I'll be sure to visit Syracuse again, that's for sure. Then he thought about Cassandra and her long, curvaceous body.

What kind of damage could she do to me, he wondered, smiling at the thoughts that played around in his head. He dried off and threw the towel around his waist, walking past the mirror. Then he noticed something; claw marks. He looked at the ten little blood marks on his back and touched them, wincing.

Steph fucking clawed my back!

"Oww! That's smarts!" He threw on one of the new shirts he bought and grabbed the rest of his clothes, throwing them on the bed. He dressed quickly, grabbing his cell phone to look up his next sexual endeavor. He walked through the room as he did so.

Mark really had to applaud Denise's taste. Dozens of time she had been here, in this resort, and she had always told him to come here. He looked around the suite, at all the rooms that it had.

It was a fucking house! You could live here comfortably and not be cramped. He liked this place. He wondered if Cassandra would. He thumbed through his phone apps. When he found the yellow page application, he started skimming the pages.

Escorts, escorts; he found it. He found the first number on it and pressed the call button. In a few moments, a woman answered.

"Accent Escort Service, this is Claudia, how may I help you today?" Mark stopped for a second, thinking of what to say.

"Yes,   I   would   like   a   female   escort." *That was simple enough.*

"Any preferences, sir?" He thought again.

What sounds good right now?

"I want a black woman, long hair, very beautiful. Is that enough or do I need to give specifics?"

Apparently he didn't. The rest was wish-wash shit like credit card numbers and when Mark wanted her, which was now. He wanted her for two hours that was all.

He still had an urge inside. Mark was sure it would take at least a couple of hours to get Cassandra to strip down so it would be at least two or three in the morning before they started fucking. For some reason, maybe since he was away from home, he wanted to fuck. He felt like he almost needed it. The lady took him off hold.

"Yes sir, she'll be there in thirty minutes. Is that acceptable?"

He said yes.

Mark waited. He was getting a sudden urge to have sex and he didn't know why. Maybe since it was somebody besides his wife he had begun to enjoy it again.

Mark sat there, watching television, waiting for the escort, when he got the urge. In moments, he was unzipping his jeans, his cock out, getting ready to masturbate when, finally, there was a knock on the door. He slid his cock back into his boxers and got up to answer the door. When he opened it, he was surprised. She was more beautiful than he imagined. This woman, Janice the escort service had told him, was very attractive, and looking at the boner sticking out of his boxers.

She walked in nonchalantly.

"I think I can guess what you want." She pointed to his cock sticking out. He blushed and pushed it back down in his pants, zipping them up. She smiled at Mark and took a good look.

"My, my. You are a real looker, you know? I really won't mind having you. That is what I'm here for, right?"

"That's correct. I need pleasure." He felt like a helpless little kid, asking for a hug from his mommy. But this wasn't his mommy. And he didn't want a hug. Janice took her clothes off immediately, which consisted merely of a long, glittering sequined dress. It fell to the floor quick, showing him what his money had bought.

"So your name is Mark, right?" She looked up at him, her naked body nearing. Mark nodded. For some strange reason, he was nervous. Mark had been with a number of women in his lifetime and he had never been nervous; well except maybe once. But he was definitely nervous right now. Maybe it was because he had never been with a black woman before.

There was a lot of competition out there in the real world and the stigma was that white men had nothing on black men, or so Mark had heard. Mark almost wanted to shy away from her but remained, answering her question without any weakness in his voice.

"Yes. Mark's fine. And your...... your name is Janice?" The black woman nodded. She was looking down at his pants, her hand on the zipper and moving inside his boxers. Her hands felt so good on his cock.

"Yes, it's Janice. And I prefer to be called that. I've never had a white man quite like you before. I hope you don't disappoint me. Right now, from the feel of it... I don't have to worry about that. What do you want me to do first? I can stroke you for a while if you like." She ran her palm across the tip of his cock. "Or I can suck your cock, or just ride you right now. You've got me. What will it be, Mark?"

"I want to feel how wet your pussy can get."

Mark laid her on the bed and entered her, pushing himself in slow and then pulling out. Janice was tight. It felt good to him though, moving in and out slowly, still standing but leaning over a bit, watching her face as he prodded her every time, moving deeper inside.

"I want you to feel this cock inside you, Janice!" She moved with his strokes, watching his face, waiting for him to come. It was quick. He could feel the pressure building within. Janice let her fingers drift down Mark's back, her fingernails dragging across his ass, making his cock stiffen inside of her even more.

"Mark, honey, what are you waiting for? Aren't you going to come? I can feel it. You're holding back. Push it out. I like myself full of come." She smacked his ass, Mark's cock throbbing from the pain and pleasure mixed together. Janice continued her dirty talk.

"Do you like me to talk dirty to you? Oh, I bet you do." She continued, seeing how Mark relished in it. She squeezed his ass and pressed him into her, her tongue lapping at the small beads of sweat on his chest. "Oh Mark, I've bet you've never fucked a black woman before either, have you?"

Mark shook his head, moving faster. She was really turning him on.

"Mark, I want you to cum inside me. Before you come, tell me. I love feeling cum explode inside me." He came then, Janice slamming his wet cock into her tight hole. Mark's load squirted inside her, the dark-skinned beauty keeping him in her until he was finished. Mark then pulled out, a few drips of his cum spilling out onto her thighs. She loved it. She raked the rest of his cum on her thighs up with her fingers and rubbed it across her chest.

"Mark, now I'm going to show you how a black woman fucks." Mark smiled, feeling her slide down onto his shaft, bouncing softly up and down, using her strong thighs to keep her going. Mark saw that she began to feel his cock rub on a spot inside of her but she ignored it the best she could, moving up and down on Mark's cock, watching him writhe and moan in pleasure. Mark closed his eyes, letting himself feel the pleasure she was giving him. He reached around her and grabbed her bare ass, plowing his cock into her, her legs shaking a bit.

That seemed to make Janice weak.

She looked down at him while she pressed her pussy down onto his cock, shoving her hips forward to feel his shaft rub against her clit. Mark slid deep inside of her and set her off, the escort bouncing down hard on him, her orgasm bursting out and down onto his thighs.

"Oh Mark! Mark, that feels so good! Do I have to stop?" She looked at him, waiting for a response. Mark was about to come and he begged for her to continue. Janice moaned liked no woman he had ever heard, slamming herself into his thighs, both of them coming at the same time. Soon, she slowed the pace down and leaned down against him, her hard nipples pressing against his chest.

"You weren't a disappointment, Mark. Be proud! Be very proud!" They continued after a brief resting period, Janice riding him until they tired themselves out. They both then collapsed on the bed, lying next to each other. Mark drifted off to sleep.

Mark awoke later that afternoon, about five, the sun in the middle of the sky outside his suite.

I *slept through Janice's leaving*. He never had a chance to say goodbye. He tried to get up.

Oh, am I sore! He lifted himself off of the bed and walked to the bathroom, looking back at the puddles left on the bed. Mark showered again. After showering, he got a new change of clothes from his shopping bags and checked his wallet for anything missing, just in case. Nothing was missing. He threw his clothes that he had worn earlier into the laundry hamper, walking back over to the phone.

He called the front desk, asking for a maid to tidy up and for his driver to be readied. Mark was out for the day again, the same old man chauffeur that he had for the latter part of yesterday. The driver tipped his hat to Mark who, in turn, smiled and slid into the backseat.

The first place he went was to a place to eat. He was starving not having eaten breakfast or lunch. It was almost time for dinner and his stomach cursed him over and over until he pulled the limo into a small fast food chicken shack. It was just like old times, except that he had never had a limo at his service. Sometimes it was a hassle to have a limo. Someone always knew where you went, where you were going. You couldn't just on the spur of the moment stop and look around. It had to be announced. But, of course, a limo did have some great advantages; like last night with Stephanie and that afternoon, when the driver had carried his bags.

Mark got a chicken box from the take-out window and got back into the limo and the limo drove off. He ate voraciously; as if he hadn't eaten in weeks, telling the chauffeur, with a mouth full of chicken, to drive to the same mall that he had gone to yesterday. They were there in no time; Mark soon finishing his meal, dropping it in the trash can near the entrance. He wiped the crumbs off his polo shirt and wiped his mouth with a napkin, disposing of that also. He carried his drink with him, eyeing all of the shops again, making his way through the many that filled the empty spaces around him.

It was Saturday night and busy inside the mall, the crowd thicker than it had been the night before. Mark made his way through the crowd easily enough, looking for the entrance to the food centre. Soon, he was there and making his way to the Golden Arch. But Stephanie was not there. There were other girls, probably her age, maybe a little younger, manning the registers.

Mark walked back out of the centre and went to the flower shop inside the mall, ordering a bouquet. He told them whom he wanted them delivered to in the mall and they had no problem with it. Steph would know it was him. Before he paid the clerk, he went to Victoria's Secret and bought a gift card for her, slipping it into the card.

She could buy something nice to keep those breasts in, he thought to himself, smiling at what he had done. It was now 6:50p.m. and the Syracuse game would be starting in less than an hour. He wondered if he could make it there in time. He had bought a Syracuse shirt and matching hat to go in and he would like to attend.

The limo driver had waited outside and stood straight out of the car when Mark came out, getting the door for him. Mark asked for the bags in the back of the trunk he had brought with him from his room and he dug through them before he got in, getting out the outfit. He climbed into the limo and told the driver where to go. Mark slipped his shirt off, replacing it with the Syracuse shirt. He changed the rest of his clothes also, slipping on a new pair of shoes and finally slipping the cap on his head. The stadium was coming up and he looked at his watch again. It was 7:20. He might just make it. He made his way to the ticket counter. The man inside stood there, pointing to the prices on the sign above him. Mark brushed the comment off.

"I'm a friend of Cassandra Leonard. She said she would have a ticket for me here at the box office." The ticket man skimmed through the pages of held tickets and pulled out two tickets, handing them to Mark through the slot in the glass window.

Two tickets? Mark didn't' know anybody else. He looked over to his chauffeur and smiled.

The chauffeur followed him in after a little bit of coaxing. First, they had to get the driver a change of clothes. Mark slid out his credit card and told the driver to get whatever he wanted to wear, as long as it was Syracuse related. The old man ended up getting a Syracuse sweatshirt and matching jogging pants, with a colorful hat like Marks. He also got a big foam hand with the words SYRACUSE # 1 printed on it. The old man, Ronald was his name, caught Mark by surprise. They had missed the kickoff but entered just as the opposing team was running the ball, Ronald finally speaking up.

"I love Syracuse! They're the best damn college team around!" Mark laughed and sat the bag with Ronald's clothes on the ground, signaling the beer man. They both drank after a little coaxing from Mark and, soon, they had their dinner on the seats, watching the game throughout the night. Mark had to admit that he hadn't had so much fun in years. Ronald turned out to be a really nice old man. He wasn't stiff like Mark thought at first. He was just a regular guy.

Mark remembered something that he had to do. He told Ronald that he'd be right back and went back to the ticket counter and left his phone # and address to his suite for Cassandra. Mark returned right at the end of the fourth quarter. Syracuse won and Ronald and Mark went back to the limo, which was still parked right in front of the stadium, like there was actually a driver in it. They made their way out quickly, Ronald not changing until they were out of the stadium's parking lot. Mark handed the old man his clothes up front. Ronald thanked him for the wonderful night as he changed in the front seat in a parking lot down the street, watching the crowd of cars whiz by them, screaming Syracuse's victory.

They soon pulled into the hotel, Ronald opening the door, now back in his suit, straightening his tie. Mark smiled and tipped him another hundred dollars.

"Tight-lipped, remember. That's how I like it." Mark made the motion of zipping up his lips and chuckled, walking into the resort. He passed by others, mostly rich pricks, and took the elevator up to his room on the top floor. He dropped the bags in his room and walked out onto the balcony. It overlooked the whole city of

Syracuse. The first night he had got there, after he dropped off Steph, he just looked out at the dazzling beauty that the city lights made, taking him back to times he remembered in his youth.

It was breathtaking up here. The air was thin but it was fresher than the shit that the people breathed on the streets, full of carbon monoxide and other pollutants. Plus, Syracuse was in the upstate part of New York, which was filled with mostly crops and small farming towns.

Mark remembered when he used to be concerned with the environment in college, striking against the government several times to abolish automobiles completely. It was hard to believe that the spoiled high school brat with the new car and free college would ever do anything like that, but he did. Mark and other protestors had set up roadblocks on the college campus, having demonstrations that proved that automobiles were toxic to the land and to people as well.

Mark jumped to a start when there was a knock on the door. It was room service.

It must be the champagne and strawberries, Mark thought, making his way to the door.

The young man pulled the cart next to the bed, asking if Mark needed anything else to let him know. Mark handed a twenty out to him and the service boy smiled, walking out with the words thank you coming out of his lips as he closed the door to Mark's suite. He needed to get ready.

It was 11:00p.m. now and Mark had an hour or so to prepare for Cassandra. He looked through the bags he had bought and pulled out the bag he was looking for.

It had all kinds of things in it: handcuffs, body lotions, edible underwear, and hot oils. He was ready. He had never used any of these and he wondered what they would be like.

Why not try now? What the hell! Mark dug through his bags and slipped the silk boxers on that he had bought, slipping the suite's bathrobe on over it, spraying a couple of mists of his favorite cologne into the air as he walked through it. The mist caught on the fabrics and stayed; a trick that his wife had taught him years ago. Mark walked into the living room of the suite and lay on the sofa, surfing through the channels. In no time, he was asleep.

It was around 12:30 a.m. when he awoke from the sofa, a light tap on the door, Mark almost falling off the sofa. He recovered and stood up, stretching, moving for the door. He opened it.

Cassandra was there; dressed in a skin-tight, tan brown body suit, showing her curves more than what she had on at the airport. Her red hair was tied up in the back, her neck completely barren with only a necklace made of crystal lying against her neck, a small series of crystals hanging down in between her breasts.

But someone was with her. It was another woman.

It looked almost like Cassandra's splitting image, only a couple of years younger. The young woman with Cassandra wore a long coat that covered a Syracuse cheerleading outfit she had on, *probably to keep fans from coming up to her. She was an original Syracuse cheerleader. What was happening here?*

When Cassandra saw the puzzled look on Mark's face she spoke, justifying everything in a couple of sentences.

"This is my younger sister, Alexis. She wanted to come with me? I hope you don't mind."

Alexis' voice piped up.

"Have you ever had a threesome?"

The night was just starting. Mark wanted to pass out, wanted to fall on his face and beg for mercy; but that wouldn't happen. He answered somewhat nervously.

"No, not yet. Is there something I need to know?"

Both sisters smiled at the same time, Alex dropping her long coat in the doorway.

My god, she looked almost as good as Cassandra, which was really hard to do.

Yes, Mark agreed to himself, *the night was only starting.*

Chapter Four

- PUBLIC DISPLAY OF AFFECTION -

Denise was at her shoot in Paris, France, watching as the fans and groupies flocked around her limo as it pulled in the studio parking lot. It almost made her sick. The studio lot was supposed to be closed off, but there were always those that allowed the fans to come in. There were fan clubs, prizes and trips that were in the contract for each actor to pose with groupies, and entertainment websites and shows that peppered all celebrities with questions that had nothing to do with the movie.

These stupid little people, don't you have your own lives, she thought. This is pathetic! She wanted to slap each one of them as she passed by, flashbulbs and microphones in her face. She wanted to flick them the bird.

Fuck you all, she would say, and would walk back into her trailer. But instead she just smiled as the limo door opened and put on her best picture face, walking back to her trailer to prepare for the continuous shooting at the studio.

It was the fourth day of the movie shoot when Denise Malone got the call.

She was in her dressing trailer, letting the hairstylists primp her hair for the erotic dance scene coming up when the phone rang. Her hair was in curlers and her nails were still wet. She was very agitated. Denise reached her hand out for the phone.

"Give me the damn phone, would you please? It's getting on my last nerve!" Her voice was piercing, like the scratching of nails on a chalkboard. Most of the people around didn't really like working with her. In fact, some of them even quit, refusing to work for a bitch like her. In reality, Denise was a bitch. She shook her hand impatiently, practically ripping the phone from the stylist's grip. She clicked the phone on. Her tone was harsh when she answered.

"Yes, this is Mrs. Malone, can I help you? I'm sort of in the middle of something." She waited for an answer. Her face softened immediately when the person on the other end spoke. She spoke for several moments, smiling and chatting then hung up with a smile on her face, her thoughts lingering to what the man had said.

Tonight, she thought. *Oh god!* She couldn't wait. She finished her part of the film they were doing and, as soon as the camera crew packed up for the night, she was in her trailer, changing into a silk blouse. She neglected the bra completely.

That's how Nathan liked it. Denise slid into matching slacks, sliding off her panties before putting them on.

He had always liked easy access to her goodies, sometimes taking her in the car on the side of the freeway.

She loved the adventurous spirit that Nathan held within, only releasing it to her during their moments of sex. Of course, he did have a girlfriend, but this wasn't something she thought of as long-term, so she didn't mind at all. She would die for a bottle of the spirit he had inside of him, paying any amount of money that he wanted. She could make a killing off that kind of business.

She walked outside the trailer and, to her surprise, he was waiting out in his GT Bentley Cabriolet for her, the top down and a bottle of wine in his hand. He motioned for her to jump in. When she climbed in, he laid the bottle in the backseat and slid a hand into her blouse, fingering her nipples. They were hard instantly, his breath on her neck, tugging at thoughts of last year when they were together. Nathan then pulled away and smiled.

He was different from other men. Yes, he did have a French accent, which was sexy all on its own, but he also had this fire inside him that seemed to drip out of every pore. His hair was still short, black and thick, but he had let his bangs grow out, a simple part in the middle, slicked back with a little styling gel.

"Like what you're wearing, Denise. It's good for what we're going to do. You want to get crazy, right? I didn't come here for something normal." He smiled at her again, that crazy smile that could keep her coming all night. Nathan pulled off the set and zoomed her out and away from the studio's lights, far away from civilization.

They were just outside of Paris and the traffic died down as they drove for what seemed like an hour. Nathan didn't say anything to her, just drove and kept his eyes straight, pedal to the floor.

He had a plan for sure, she thought, another small city coming into view in front of them. He pulled off on the exit and drove through a couple of smaller streets, evidently planning this ahead of time. Nathan stopped on Carveen Street and pulled into a parking spot next to a strip club, uncorking the bottle of wine in the backseat and taking a long pull off of it. Denise waited for him to gulp down the mouthful before asking.

"What the hell are we doing here? I don't like this place, Nate! I hope you don't think I'm going in there." Nate smiled at her and opened his door, shutting it behind him.

"Fine. You don't have to go. Just wait out here for me. I'll be back in an hour or two." He laughed and went in, not looking back or saying anything more to her. The sun was already down and darkness had set all over the small town.

The strip club was called the Pink Pussycat. It was flashing in big, bright letters on a neon sign bolted to the top of the roof, pink and white the only thing that could be seen for miles on the lonely road. Several men walked by the car, eyeing Denise and what she wore, her nipples hard from the cold, showing through her blouse.

Looks like a classy crowd, Denise joked, flipping the strangers the bird. She got out of the car.

Dammit Nathan, she thought, opening the door to the Pink Pussycat. She paid the cover charge and slipped past the guys who were eyeing her earlier outside, a roomful of tables with men scattered throughout the area.

Nearly all of the women were attractive, close to gorgeous, in fact, Denise remarked, watching as a nearby blond dipped herself down onto a table, the dancing pole between her breasts, her tongue pressing against the cold metal. The stripper smiled. Denise couldn't help but smile back.

Denise looked around the room for Nathan. He was at the front, at the main walkway in the middle of the strip club, a tall brunette with a tiger tattoo on her left hip stripping for him and many other individuals, Nathan holding a bill out to her with his teeth. The woman thrust her backside in his face and leaned herself forward, collecting the bill with her ass cheeks, pressing them against Nathan's face before she sauntered over to the next man.

Denise watched for a while, a couple of dancers passing through the main walkway, noticing Nathan take a liking to one. When the stripper stepped off the stage, Nathan was at her side. He handed her several bills, pointing to a small booth in the corner of the club, hand on her naked ass, leading her quickly over.

She looked nothing like Denise, she noted, the petite, curvy little school-girl type that only old men like apparently getting Nathan's attention. The young stripper had short blond hair that was not tied up in pigtails, though it was in a ponytail on the back of her head. She wore the Catholic school girl outfit that gets every man who's ever fantasized about short skirts immediately hard and her face still had that softness that youth gives it.

Denise waited to see what Nathan was going to do, feeling a wetness starting to form between her legs from thinking about the things he could do to that little girl. Denise knew how much Nathan liked short hair. That's what had attracted him to her; but that was years ago.

Nathan lay back on the pillows in the booth, letting the school girl stripper climb on top of him, grinding her crotch into his. He closed his eyes and let her rub her hands all over his body, her hands stopping at his zipper. Nathan nodded in agreement, his eyes still closed. He had a smile on his face.

"That son of a bitch!" Denise wasn't about to have him spent on some cheap thrill. She had to put a stop to this.

Denise went over to them. The dancer was unzipping Nathan's pants when Denise got there, the young girl stopping when Denise stepped into the booth.

Nathan opened his eyes and smiled even wider. Denise was turned on. She heard the music playing, saw the flesh that was tempting and thought, for a moment, how much she wanted Nathan to ram his cock into her, plunging it in and out as hard as he could.

But his games were different, more complex.

He liked for women to fight over him, to flaunt themselves in front of him. He liked a show. Denise smiled.

He wants a show, huh? I'll give him a show. She unbuttoned her khaki pants and let them drop to the floor, keeping her high heels on. She slipped the shirt over her head, nipples sticking out at him, and approached slowly. The stripper just watched, as if amazed that a customer would actually do that. Then Denise pushed the stripper aside, mounting Nate herself. She danced for him. He smiled when she continued with what the stripper had started with. She slid his pants off. Patrons of the club were looking now, but Denise didn't care. She needed Nate's cock inside of her, if only for just a moment.

She hadn't felt him in her in over a year and she yearned for him to offer it to her. But he didn't so she had to do it herself. His underwear was off, too, the stripper just staring as the two individuals before her started fucking, rigorous thrusts, one after another.

When his thickness slid in, Denise let out a moan of relief. It couldn't be heard for the music but Nate could feel it vibrate through her and into him, the naked man in the strip club grabbing for the starlets' hips, quickening her pace.

He must've felt something, she thought, watching as a small crowd gathered round, watching them instead of the girls that danced onstage.

They should ask for tips, Denise thought, plunging Nathan deeper and deeper into her, her wetness melting out onto him. Nathan was into it now, sitting up, his rhythms hard and exact. She grabbed his shoulders, feeling her orgasm pulse from within, smacking her ass down on his thighs, pounding down on him just the way he liked it.

"Nathan, you bastard! Fuck me, fuck me harder! You're making me come!" She exploded, not stopping, the pleasure apparent on his face as well. He grabbed her ass and pressed himself into her as hard as he could, releasing gush after gush of pleasure, keeping himself inside of her until the pleasure subsided.

The crowd was in awe. It was as if they were at the movies and getting a free show.

I had definitely started trouble. Nathan had the look on his face now. Denise missed that look so much. She pressed his head to her chest, her bare body slick and shiny with a slight layer of perspiration. She could feel his thickness inside her.

Yes, she thought, *I definitely started something.*

Denise lifted herself off of him when the man patted her on the shoulder, handing her clothes from off of the floor. She was out of breath and dripping from her orgasm.

She slid into her pants and turned just in time to hear applause from every customer and stripper that were watching, buttoning several buttons as she was escorted out of the club, Nathan following soon after. They were both sweaty, slippery from the other's desire. Nathan gave her a smirk and jumped over the door into his seat, starting the engine. Denise buttoned the rest of her blouse and got into the car, looking over at her lover.

Damn, he was good. She hadn't ever done that before. She would be sure to write that down for things to do again in the near future. A public place was the thing she hated most. But in there,

there were no cameras or paparazzi watching her every move and making her always fearful about being followed.

Nathan drove her back to her studio trailer and followed her in, continuing with his game. She was up against the dining table, her hands braced against the wall, taking his full thrusts, moaning in pleasure as he slammed into her from behind, his hands firmly planted on her hips. She was dripping now with sweat and pleasure, Nate turning her on more than ever.

Denise turned back around when she was through with her pleasure, licking her juices off of Nathan, sliding his sex in between her breasts and into her mouth.

He tasted sweet, like strawberries, taking just the first few inches into her mouth fast and quick. He leaned back against the trailer, watching the movie star on her knees.

"Suck it, Denise! I know you've wanted this. Here it is." He didn't last long. He was a weaker man than the others that she had. He was too sensitive. He came quickly, not holding back. He was just a boy to her. She was in her late thirties now and this young twenty-three year old was like a piece of crème cake, filling her mouth with sweetness. She liked him very much, though. She couldn't deny that. It made her feel good that she could still keep up with the younger crowd.

He wasn't the biggest in size, but he did know ways that could turn her on and make her weak, a complete opposite from Mark.

My husband was a Popsicle.

Sure, he had size in his favor but he wasn't adventurous like this young fellow she was banging in between takes. She had many lovers, all across the globe, her husband Mark not knowing anything about them. She kept them secret, but always had them at her beck and call. Even this little Nathan was at her call. He stood up near her, rubbing his cock between her legs. He was hard again, pushing urgently against her insides.

I could handle more, she thought, still feeling the last orgasm she had just start to fade inside her body. The night continued, young Nathan filling her with what he had, which was just fine with her.

Chapter Five

- SOME DON'T NEED RESUMES -

The next day at the movie set was hectic. Denise's male co-star got in a brawl with four cameramen that were following him to his trailer in between scenes. The cameramen were chased away but not before they got their own licks in. One of them broke her co-star's nose. The shooting had to be postponed, so most of the cast left, including the swollen-faced Denuvo Green. He was furious, practically throwing his luggage at his chauffeur as he made his way to the limo, stomping all the way.

Denise watched all this from her trailer window, the afternoon going to shit in seconds.

The whole week had been a waste, she thought to herself, packing her things up, her plane ticket sitting on the kitchenette counter. She was going back home for a week or so, probably spend some time with Mark or something. The thought of that practically made her sick, spending time with that slug that just sits around all day.

He probably hasn't even moved from the spot at the pool, she thought again, shoving her make-up bag into her suitcase. All he had done since she had made it big in the movies was sit around. He didn't paint for anyone anymore or even paint for the hell of it, his art room and the supplies that lay in it covered over with an inch of dust it had been so long. The door was locked to the room anyway and Mark was the only one who had the key.

Denise watched as her limo arrived minutes later, the chauffeur knocking on the door. She smiled. It was Emmett, her favorite driver. He was a thick fellow, round and plump, sort of like Santa Claus. That's how she remembered him, with his graying beard and rosy cheeks. He knocked again, his tailored jacket nearly bursting at the seams. Emmett was the only person Denise could seem to stomach nowadays, with the exception of her flings. She opened the door and smiled at the older man.

"Hello, Emmett. I'll be ready to go to the airport in just a few minutes." He had a dumb look on his face, like all men get when they don't know how to say something. He apparently had something on his mind.

"Mrs. Malone. Actually, I was told by Mr. Drindden to come and get you and take you to his office at the other side of the studio before taking you to the airport." Denise finished packing her bags and let Emmett take them, getting into the white limo, cautious now to say anything.

What did Mr. Drindden want, anyway? The director barely spoke to any of the actors after the shootings unless there was a good reason.

Was it about what happened with Denuvo Green, her co-star, maybe? Was he going to fire him? She sat staring out the window while different studio buildings passed by, letting the questions build up in her head, all of them getting ready to burst out from her ears. Emmett stopped and let her out.

It was a tall building; something to the effect of the Empire state building, yet much smaller in stature when compared to it. Studios didn't really have any tall buildings but this one was up there. On the sets in the morning, if it was an open set and not in a confined lot, you could see this very building spiraling up towards the clouds above, almost touching them. She had always wondered what this building was and now she was going to find out. Emmett led her into the lounge inside, through to the elevators. Everywhere you looked the walls were decorated with posters and advertisements from different movies over the decades.

Even one of her posters was up, in a frame, the frame lights blinking around it. The place was really gaudy, all in all. She would never decorate a place with this shit, especially a building as big as this one, with all of its prestige that it has on the outside. They made it to the elevators, riding up one almost to the top of the large structure. It stopped at the 10th floor. The elevator doors opened. There was an office, a huge one at that, with a long desk and several secretaries behind it.

All of them were bimbos, of course, with big breasts and revealing clothes that helped you imagine the bra size they wore.

It was just like in some sleazy sex book or something, Denise thought. *They might as well have been naked for how much skin they showed,* laughing to herself, the memory of last night popping into her mind.

There were plush, velvet chairs and high-backed chairs that held many other clients, apparently waiting for a time to see Mr. Drindden. Emmett smiled at her and led her to a secretary, pointing in Denise's direction.

"Yes, this is Mrs. Renfield-Malone. She has an appointment to see Mr. Drindden right away. She's getting ready to leave on her flight home." The secretary paged Mr. Drindden and he confirmed it, the secretary getting up from her desk and showing Denise to his door. Emmett waved goodbye and waited in a nearby chair, picking up a magazine from the rack.

Mr. Drindden's office was enormous, which matched the size of the building; large glass windows behind his desk, looking out over the whole of the studio. There were two leather sofas parallel to each other that lined up with the sides of his desk, which was cluttered with papers, Mr. Drindden skimming through mounds and mounds of scripts for new movies. A huge bear rug rested in between the two sofas, the head facing out toward the double doors that Mrs. Renfield-Malone had come through. He stopped his reading for a moment and motioned for her to sit on one of the couches, pushing the papers on his desk aside to speak to her. The secretary left then, shutting the doors behind her.

Mr. Drindden was an older man, in his fifties, who used to be an attractive man when he was young. Now there were wrinkles on top of wrinkles and he was balding on top, not to mention that he had let his body go to waste. He had a little stomach that stuck out over his trousers and belt, propping itself comfortably on his lap. When he spoke, the most annoying voice exited his mouth, almost like he had stolen somebody else's voice and kept it for himself.

"I brought you here to speak about what happened today. You know with Mr. Denuvo Green and his attitude. I don't like those kinds of things happening. It gives the actor a bad name and it gives the director who cast them a bad name, too. Mrs. Malone, you will no longer be working with Mr. Green on this movie. He's fired."

Whoah! That was a shocker for her. She expected that but not so blunt.

"And so are you." Mr. Drindden looked back down at his paperwork, waiting for her to leave. Denise stood up, objecting as soon as the words passed his lips. She saw it in his eyes when he asked her to have a seat.

That prick!

"Why am I fired for Denuvo's mistakes? I shouldn't be punished for what some foreign actor does. What the hell is your reason?" She was upset now, her breath coming in gasps, her chest heaving up and down. Drindden noticed this.

"Because you've had a bad reputation since you first came on this set four weeks ago. I've been getting complaints left and right about you bad mouthing the make-up crew, the cameramen, even the stunt extras because they don't do things right. Mrs. Malone, I'm the director. I direct. You're the actress, you act. You don't tell my people how to run things around here. Do you hear me? Now sit your ass down!"

Denise was at a loss for words. She hadn't expected to be fired. Sure, she was tough on people. She couldn't be nice to them or they'd take advantage of her. She sat down and crossed her legs, waiting.

What now?

"You're a great actress, Denise, but you're career is going to go to shit if this attitude persists. You may have acting talent, spirit, and a great body, but that can get you only so far in Hollywood." Drindden sat back in his plush chair, pulling out a stack of papers. He dropped them on the table in front of him. It was her contract.

She couldn't just leave. That would mean defeat and she couldn't have that. In her mind sparked a plan. She stood back up, her voice breaking the silence.

"What if I change my attitude? What then? Can I come back to the set next week?" Drindden shook his head. Denise rounded his desk, coming to stand beside his chair. Her breasts were within eye view and he turned to say something to her, his words catching in his throat.

"Mrs. Malone, what are you doing behind my desk?" She slid her panties off and threw them on top of his papers, turning his chair to face her. She got on her knees and began undoing his belt, unzipping Drindden's pants. He looked as though he wanted to stop her but didn't, the bulge in his pants now in control. She pulled out his cock. For an older man, he was well hung. It wasn't as big as others she had seen, but it didn't really matter right now. She took it in her mouth. Drindden wiggled in his chair. She sucked on it hard, her hand moving up and down his shaft. She stopped and looked up at him.

"Now, what were you saying about firing me? Is that what you really want to do, Mr. Drindden? I'm sure I'll be a good girl from now on. I promise." She stood up leaned herself against the old man, sinking down onto his cock, pushing it inside of her with one firm thrust. He felt nice, sort of like a smooth massage. She could tell he was in heaven, lying back as far as he could so he could get the full feeling. He came in moments, moaning like a baby, grabbing her shoulders tightly with his hands.

Mrs. Malone kept tempting him, though, sitting on his cock, moaning and panting, as if his thing had done something no man's had done before. She pleaded with the old man to stop in her best 'fuck me' voice but he kept going, excited that he aroused her, laying her on his oak table, pushing the papers off of his desk. He was still fucking her, pumping away, when she felt something tingle in her pussy. His cock was inside of her and he was standing up, slamming into her wetness, when the feelings of an orgasm hit her. She was surprised at first, but as she felt the pulses through her body, she sat up, looking at the old man with a smile on her face. A smile of pleasure.

Denise closed her eyes and wrapped her arms around Drindden's neck, plunging him deeper into her, hitting the little pleasure spot that he had found in her. She started moving faster, his rhythms too slow to keep up to her feeling inside. Then she came, moaning hard and loud, bouncing up and down on his cock. He let his second orgasm out, squeezing her ass as he pushed her far onto the table, a puddle forming under her, on his desk, papers sticking to her bare ass. He bit onto her shoulder to stifle another moan, riding the way of his orgasm into her, rocking back and forth lightly as he came inside her.

They both stayed motionless for a time, catching their breath, looking around at the mess they had made that had fallen onto the floor. Soon, their pleasures subsided and they began straightening their clothes, Denise sliding her panties back on in front of him. He was sitting in his chair, his pants on but still not yet zipped, watching as she finished dressing. He had a grin on his face.

"Well, Denise, your husband sure is a lucky man. He knows that, doesn't he?" Drindden didn't give her time to respond.

"Well, tell him that when you see him next, okay. Fine, Mrs. Malone. You can have your job back. I just don't want to hear any more complaints about you from others, is that clear?" She nodded.

"Or I'll be right back up here to see you, isn't that right, Mr. Drindden?" She smiled back at him and left, Mr. Drindden watching her, the double doors closing, his mouth dry from hiring her back.

Denise walked out of his office and joined back up with Emmett, leaving in the limo for the airport. She held the ticket in her hand, thinking about what she had just done.

Was that wrong, or what? Well, at least she didn't have to worry about that slut Clarise getting her job. She chuckled when the idea of poor Clarise trying to top what she had just done. Denise knew she had left that old man a fond spot in his memory of her for ages to come. Denise had a few more movies in her contract but was almost finished, her thoughts lingering to other deals.

She left at her shoot in Paris to her home in Beverly Hills. She couldn't wait to get home and relax in her Jacuzzi, having her husband bring her drinks.

That's how it should be, she thought, looking out the window of the plane, the scenery moving by, clouds all around her. Denise laid back and soon, was fast asleep in her first class seat, blanket around her. She was awakened by a familiar voice in her ear, whispering her name. It was Nathan.

"Denise, just keep your eyes closed. The flight attendants think you're asleep. I came to see you at your trailer and you had already left. I couldn't wait until next week when you returned. I had to see you." His hand slid down under the covers, slithering under her dress, pulling at her panties.

Keeping her eyes closed, Denise lifted up like she was getting comfortable, feeling Nathan slide her panties down to mid-thigh.

The blanket covered her fully, from her shoulders to her high heels, the width of it covering the other seat next to her as well. That's where Nathan sat now, pretending to be asleep also, his fingers entering her. He began moving them in and out, rubbing on her insides, making her wet. Denise began to get excited, a soft moan escaping her lips. Nathan quickened his hand, fingers moving hard and fast, her legs closing in on his hand.

"Go faster", she whispered, which was too much. She came on his hand, fingers dripping with juices, her breath throaty and course, her legs still tight around his hand as she bit her lip to contain the moan meant for him. Denise then reached for Nathan, stroking his bulge from the outside of his pants. Denise unzipped and reached inside.

Chapter Six

- NO REST FOR THE WICKED -

That night Mark woke up, the door closing behind the two sisters. He went to stand up. His hand was stuck to something. He looked over at the headboard.

The handcuffs had gone to good use. Things around him were still blurry from the champagne, Mark watching everything spin before his eyes. He looked around for the key. It was there, on the writing desk, about five feet away. There was no way he could reach it. He laid back down on the bed, his head throbbing, his mind a blur of memories. He could still see the two come at him, almost as if they were crazed animals devouring his flesh. Cassandra's sister had done this before apparently, many times, with other men and women. But Mark didn't mind in the least.

An experience he would never forget. He could still smell them on him. Their scent would probably linger in this room for days, unlike Janice's which was not nearly as strong as the two sisters that left Mark cuffed to the bed. Cassandra had turned out to be the weaker of the two, moaning and almost bursting into tears when he gave her her first orgasm, watching the pleasure in her face from above, her sister wanting him next. Cassandra had said to Mark that it was Alex's idea from the start. Cassandra was planning a nice, quiet dinner for the two when Alex was released from the game and caught up with her sister. She said that Alex had a sex appetite like no one else. And Mark could now see why.

*   *   *

Alex was a little bit rougher with her men, the cheerleading dress now off, revealing her smooth, tanned thighs and firm, round ass. She looked a lot like her older sister in certain aspects, all except for the length of her hair and the texture. She was the first to experiment with the hot oils. As Cassandra slid off the bed, Alex climbed on, squeezing a handful of the hot oil into her hands. She rubbed it on Mark's chest and stomach, moving down to his thighs.

That's where she stayed most of the time, her mouth tearing at him, making him reach for her, trying to keep her at bay. As the oil sank into his skin, it began to heat up. His entire body felt as if it were on fire, making him go wild with desire. He pulled at Alex and she came up at him, swinging her shapely legs over his burning body. Then she pulled out the handcuffs.

*   *   *

His handcuffed arm was sore now, a redness starting to show at the wrist. He looked around at the room, shadows cast about in different places, as well as in far corners. He reached for the phone. The desk clerk answered.

"Yes, could you send my driver up here with the room key, please? There are some things I need him to carry down." It cost Mark another hundred but Ronald got the handcuff keys and let him loose in less than an hour, Mark trying his best to rub the soreness out of his wrist. Mark thought, for some reason, that Ronald was beginning to enjoy working for him. Ronald left then, walking out of the suite, shaking his head and letting out a little laugh as he let the door shut behind him.

Mark fell back onto the bed, looking over at the clock.

Five a.m. It's almost time for me to leave. Just another few hours and he'd have to be on the plane again, another tourist attraction in mind.

He had enough of Syracuse to last him at least a couple of months. Now he was off to Washington D.C.

He smiled and rubbed the soreness out of his wrist, dropping the handcuffs on the floor by the bed. He drifted off to sleep.

Later that morning, he awoke to a knock on his door. It was Ronald. He could hear the old man's voice through the door, tapping lightly with his knuckles.

"Mr. Malone. I think we need to leave. We have two hours until the flight leaves. Mr. Malone, are you awake?" Mark called out a reply, gradually opening the door, his eyes still half-shut. Ronald laughed again. Marked tried to give him a smile but he was too tired. He walked into the bathroom and started the shower. Ronald started a conversation while gathering up Mark's things to leave.

"You know, Mr. Malone, you're probably the most exciting client I've ever had the pleasure to chauffeur around. I never have been offered anything like that from other people," speaking in detail about the Syracuse game the night before. Mark replied in return, scrubbing his body with soap, trying his best to get the oil out of the pores of his skin.

"I had a fun time, too, Ronald. I hope we can do this again sometime. I really appreciate what you've done for me. Not many limo drivers are as laid back as you." Mark was out of the shower now and was drying off. Ronald was grabbing up the shopping bags that Mark had acquired over the last couple of days and began taking them to the limo. Mark dressed quickly, looking at his watch.

Oh shit! Less than two hours until the flight departs!

He knew that with all the security one had to go through at the airport, he would barely make it. He slid his shoes on and grabbed the remainder of the bags and shut the door behind him.

It was a bright autumn day in Syracuse that Mark left, looking out of the limousine window, watching as the hotel disappeared from sight, Ronald quiet while on the way there. All of Mark's bags were now in a collection of shipping boxes in the trunk, folded neatly, the boxes labeled. Ronald had seen to that. Mr. Malone rolled down the window of the limo, the warm sun shining down on his face, soon drifting him off to sleep. He had an eventful past couple of days.

It seemed to show in him now though; Mark on the leather seats, feet stretched out across the limo to the other seats. It was nearly half an hour later when Ronald pulled up at the airport, unloading the boxes at the outside check-in counter, a nearby Skycap official taking them off his hands. He thanked them and knocked on the window of the limo.

Ronald was standing there, door opened, the airport in view. Mark stepped out, stretching his sore limbs. He reached for his wallet. Ronald shook his head.

"Mr. Malone, this one's on me. I insist. You've been a kind person. I have something for you. I saw that you were going to D.C., so...." Ronald pulled out a small sealed envelope from his inside coat pocket and gave it to Mr. Malone. Mark put it in his pocket and shook Ronald's hand, reaching for his wallet once again. Ronald protested but Mark insisted. He pulled out his business card and gave it to the limo driver. The old man smiled when he read it.

"I knew you were an artist. Could tell by your hands."

"Call me sometime when you're in my area. Maybe we can get together and go see a football game or whatever." Mark walked into the airport.

The Syracuse airport was just as busy as it had been when he arrived just days ago, almost the exact amount of travelers bustling to get their bags from the baggage claim. He saw the spot where he had met Cassandra. Mark smiled.

She was definitely something; he smiled to himself, walking onward to his terminal. He was still sore from last night's escapades with her and her sister, but he felt better after his shower. He walked to a small airport shop and bought some bottled water and a magazine. He drank from the bottle immediately.

Those women drained me of all of my fluids! He was tired, achy; almost too tired to move. He definitely overworked himself that time. He wished he could have one night where he could just sleep; a comfortable bed, a nice cool room and even cooler sheets that he could drift to sleep on. That would make his week. He made it just in time for departure. They seated him in first class, the flight attendant getting him another bottle of water and took his empty one from him. The flight took off as scheduled, lifting off the ground, his body sinking into the first class seat he had reserved. He put on some headphones the flight attendant had given him and relaxed, skimming through the magazine. Then, in moments, he drifted off to sleep, the hour and a half flying by just as the plane did, landing softly in the Dulles airport, Mark waking when the flight attendant shook him slightly.

"Sir, the flight's over. All of the other passengers are off the plane. It's time to leave." He looked up at her through sleepy eyes and nodded.

I need to get some rest, he thought again, lugging his on-flight bags to the baggage claim. There, another chauffeur met him, holding a sign up with Mark's name on it. Mark stopped in front of him and dropped his bags, shaking the driver's hand.

"I'm Arthur. I'll be your driver while you're here in D.C. I hope you enjoy it here." Arthur was an older man, about fifty, just a little younger than Ronald. He had black hair that was mixed with little speckles of white in it and towered over Mark, smiling down at him.

"Mr. Malone, you look exhausted! Bad flight?" Mark shook his head. The truth just seemed to ooze out of him.

"Too many women. I can't take anymore. I am just out of it. You know what I mean?" Arthur seemed a little uncomfortable with the question but laughed when he saw the lazy expression on Mark's face. He was dead serious. Arthur took his bags and led him outside to the limo where he opened the door and let Mark inside. It was cool in the back. The seats were material and not the sticky leather like the other limo he had ridden in only hours ago.

He drifted off while Arthur went to get his other baggage. The ride was comforting. Arthur didn't disturb Mark, just followed the directions he had gotten with the pick-up instructions. It was about half an hour before Arthur pulled up at the Hilton, opening the door. Mark got out, a little bit more refreshed than their first meeting. He tipped Arthur and the bellboys that gathered his things, Mark walking in with his water and magazine. The night was over. Mark hit the bed and was out the rest of the night.

But the next day started with a bang.

One of his clients from D.C. was trying to find him and, when they knew that Mark was in town, the client called immediately. It was 8:oo a.m. when the first call went through to Mr. Malone's room. He lay there, in the bed, still fully dressed, looking at the phone as it rang for the umpteenth time, finally reaching for it. It was the hotel clerk downstairs. He had remembered his voice from last night when he checked in. He was young and had a scratchy voice, as if he hadn't yet reached puberty. There was a call for him.

"Well, who is it?" Mark was already irritated. He could sleep another day if he wanted to. Then the desk clerk connected his call with the client. The voice pierced his heart, made him sit up in bed. It was Jessica, his old fiancée.

"Mark, I've been trying to get in touch with you for months now. Why haven't you returned my calls?" Mark was at a loss for words.

Calls? He hadn't received any messages from Jessica. He spoke.

"You didn't call at my house, did you? Tell me you called at my office." She sat there for moments, without responding, and then spoke up.

"I tried your office but they said you were on an "extended vacation", as they called it. They said they didn't know when you'd be back. I told them it was important and they gave me the number to your house. I've called several times but either you weren't there or the butler said he would take a message and, I guess, never gave it to you. Why? Can't I call you at your house? I am still your client, aren't I?"

She used her pouty voice on him. It always worked. Mark had pretty much ruled her out as a client when she left California, probably some three years ago. After that, he hadn't heard much from her. He had always been close to her, mostly just in the ways of emotional support. He didn't like to think of her as one of his lays. She was more than that. At least, he hoped she was.

He replied, trying not to really address the issue of her being a client or not.

"So, why did you call, Jessica? Do you need a painting done or anything? Because if you do, I can't help; at least not right now. I'm done with that. They told you right; I'm on a vacation of sorts. All of my clients have been referred to other artists. But I can refer you to a really good artist in D.C. that I know." She seemed to stray from that conversation.

"I really just wanted to see you again, Mark. I know you're married but I just wanted to spend some time with you, you know, like we used to those years ago. Do you have any time I could have?" He didn't want to answer.

Yet, somehow, he knew he would agree. She had a way of making people fall to her needs. But he wondered what she really wanted. It couldn't just be to talk. She said she had been calling him for a month now. What could be so important?

"Okay, we can meet. But I'm on vacation, Jessica. Give me a few days to rest while I'm here." He knew she would agree to that. He made up some story, that he had to do some other things before he met her and she agreed.

They would meet at a public place; Dargini's. It was an Italian restaurant, not far from the Maryland border, with good food and ever better wines. He hadn't had wine since he'd gotten married. That would work out good. He fell back asleep after he told the clerk to hold his calls and give him a wake-up call at 11:30, just a couple of hours from now.

His mind lingered with memories of Jessica and their relationship together, from their first kiss to their first time in bed. Both had been virgins at the time and it was during their high school years.

*   *   *

They were just stupid sophomores in Grant's East High School in California. She was an avid book reader and he was a long-time surfer, wandering the beaches after school, sometimes during school, not really interested in education at all. He seemed to take pleasure in the world around him and the things that it provided. His father was a rich executive at a major law firm at the time and his mother a full-time nurse at the local hospital just miles from where they lived. Both pretty much provided everything that he wanted; his surfing equipment and a t.v. in the summertime and his convertible mustang when school was in.

That's how he had met her. He was cruising, just learning how to drive, when she walked in his path, almost hitting her. She shook a balled-up fist at him and he apologized immediately, not liking enemies, especially women. He followed her up the street, trying to make it up to her. He asked her if she wanted a ride. She said no several times, but he wouldn't leave, Jessica finally giving into his kindness. Then his mind drifted to months later.

They were on his couch, Jessica coming to his house after school to help him study geometry. She was really into it but, for some reason, he couldn't concentrate. She had a summer top on with spaghetti straps that kept falling off her thin shoulders; if it wasn't one side, it was the other. Mark kept staring at her smooth skin, then at her neck, his eyes running down into her shirt, following the curves. He tried not to stare but he couldn't help it. This was the first young woman that wasn't interested in him. Then she noticed him looking. She covered her chest with her hands.

"Mark, what are you staring at? Forget it, I'm leaving." She got up to leave, putting her books and things in her bag. Mark could tell that she was embarrassed. Her cheeks were a bright red and she held one of her hands to her chest as she finished packing up. He stood up next to her and ran his fingers across her bare back, going up to her neck, wrapping one arm around her so she couldn't leave. Then he placed his mouth on her neck, sinking his teeth softly in.

She melted in his arms, her hands pushing his mouth harder against the soft skin of her neck as she pulled him closer. Mark moved his hands inside of her summer top, across the smooth skin of her tummy and to her bra, which he had unfastened in moments. Her nipples were hard and she let out a tiny moan when he touched them, rubbing her body against his. He turned her around. Their lips touched. She went into a frenzy, eyes glazed over with something he hadn't ever seen in her eyes before; passion.

She let Mark take off her clothes. Both of them were shaking, holding each other, rubbing their hands against the other, mouths going wild. She was small and petite, but smooth and soft. He kissed all over her bare body, biting at her skin, smelling the fragrance that issued forth as she began to perspire, using all of his senses, driving himself mad as well as her. She wanted to go further but her innocence didn't allow it. She was naked on the couch, Mark hovering over her, getting ready to enter her. She stopped him and sat up, putting her clothes back on. Tears were in her eyes and she avoided his face.

"I'm sorry, Mark, but I can't do this! I really want to but I'm scared. Please don't tell anyone, okay?" She left, tears streaking her face, trying to compose herself as she as she walked out the door and down the street, back to her house miles away. Mark sat there for some time, wondering what had gone wrong.

What the fuck happened?

From then on they had just stayed to being friends, talking and going out places with each other for company. That day never entered their conversations. It wasn't until days away from high school graduation that Jessica came over to give some invitations out to his parents. His parents had taken a liking to her from the start, complimenting her after she left, telling Mark that he should go after her.

If they only knew.

He was upstairs, unknowingly beginning on his first masterpiece that would that would send his career soaring, when she came in. She was decked out in her graduation gown, swirling around for him to see. He gave a mock whistle, applauding when she did her final turn. She gave him an invitation.

"Open it now. I want you to see it." Mark wiped the paint from his hands with a paintbrush rag nearby and took the invitation, opening it.

It was an invitation, alright. And, in it, was a condom. It had his name on the package. Jessica came up to him slowly, sitting on his lap while he still sat in his chair. She grabbed his hands and led them under her graduation robes, to her bare skin, which was covered with chill bumps.

She wasn't wearing any clothes underneath! She leaned over to him and held him close for a couple of moments, whispering in his ear.

"I want you to be my first. I'm leaving for college the day after graduation and I don't know if I'll ever see you again. I'm sorry for what happened those years ago. You scared me when you touched me. I've never felt that before. Nobody ever really wanted me. Will you still have me?"

Mark was dating someone at the time and it was beginning to get serious. In fact, his girlfriend was ready to have sex. But Jessica was there, now, the one that he really wanted. He slid off her robe and began caressing her body, watching her eyes close, her head tilting back. She was so soft, tender, and her touch burned for days afterward, as if her touch was pure fire. And it must have been. They were in bed for hours, Jessica's body shaking with pleasure, the door locked just in case.

But his parents weren't stupid, they knew. They had probably planned this in the first place. That was their first and last time. He would never forget that.

Chapter Seven

- MEMORIES OF YESTERYEAR —

It was 11:29 a.m. on the clock by his bed when the phone rang again. Mark sat up and grabbed the receiver, confirming the wake-up call. He put the receiver back down, lifting himself off of the bed. He looked around. The sun was coming out and it shined in through the window onto the floor and on most of his bed. He looked over at the boxes, sluggishly walking over to them.

He sifted through several of them, picking out a pair of jeans and, finally, and an Eddie Bauer long sleeve shirt. He changed in the bathroom; doing all of his grooming as quickly as his tired body would go, finishing off by straightening his belt. He left then, his mind on the things that the city held for him.

History. He never liked history and really didn't give a shit about famous dead people, as long as they stayed where they were.

I don't need any zombie apocalypses to keep me busy.

But the beauty of the monuments and the time that it had taken to create each one captured Mark's true love for art.

The day was beautiful, shining down on Mark, Arthur, and the others around them as they walked the paved streets and sidewalks to the Lincoln Memorial. Behind them, the Washington Monument jutted up in all its beauty. Mark stood there for the longest time, finally climbing over the restriction ropes to touch it. It was smooth, like marble, and it was warm from the sunlight beating down upon it. All of these sights inspired him, made him breathe in the beauty through his eyes. Then he thought of Jessica.

She was beautiful to me, also. She had always been. Maybe that's why he couldn't be with her.

*   *   *

After Jessica went to college, Mark became a wild man. He partied every night, waking up with someone different most mornings. He didn't care anymore. His art and women seemed to be the only thing on his mind, his grades dropping drastically. He had lost respect for women and, through his eyes, they were just pleasure for the taking.

And he took it.

But then the Christmas holiday rolled around, Jessica calling him to say she was coming down.

Great, he thought, pushing off the girlfriends he had at the time. He made room for her at his apartment, making his roommates get their act together, and it wasn't long before she arrived, her bags in his room. She was surprised to see him, he could tell. He looked different, though. She hugged him and gave him a soft kiss, sitting on his bed.

"So, tell me what you've been up to." She waited for his answer. It was apparent on his face. She could see the answer already. He hadn't waited for her. Mark was already over her and up to the tricks that his roommates had encouraged upon him. She left two days later, going back to college, not even spending Christmas with him. That's when things began to change.

It was just after Christmas, on New Year's Eve, when Mark met Denise. She was a little bit tipsy and so was he, both of them watching the clock eagerly at the local bar, waiting for the second hand to hit the 12. When it did, they bumped into each other, his lips sliding across her cheek. She closed her eyes for the moment, feeling the softness, then turned to Mark and planted one on him. That's how it started.

*   *   *

He was scared of Jessica, of the love she had for him, of what she could offer him that others couldn't. He wasn't ready for that. But life seemed to get in the way and Denise had an effect on him that he couldn't get away from. They got married a couple of years later after dating for a while. Everyone told them they made the perfect couple. They never had children; mostly because there was never time for any. Denise had suddenly jumped into movies and struck gold, traveling to places all over the world to do each movie, spending months at a time away. Sometimes he went, but mostly he just stayed at home, painting until he tired of it. He had no more inspiration. His life was void of anything except for staying in the house or going out with his wife and the rest of the cast in her movies, to the premiere or some other ring-ding affair.

Mark and Arthur stopped at a concession booth to eat after seeing the Lincoln Memorial, grabbing a hot dog and some chips. They washed it down with an ice-cold soda. The rest of the day was like this, traveling from one tourist attraction to the other, Mark taking notes for inspiration in a notepad. They spent all day outside and, when the city was finally
blanketed in night and stars hung over them, they went to Union Station, the last one on their list to visit. It was spectacular.

High, domed ceilings blanketed them like a tent and dozens of guards stood at each entrance, with a weapon and shield, watching the beautiful attraction from above the doors. There were people taking pictures, others just staring, but Mark sketched it in his notepad. His ink pen slid across the paper and caught the knight's face, bending around for his shield that stood almost as tall as the solemn figure itself. He drew others, capturing their grim visages on paper, drawing every detail that he could get on the small, hand-sized notepad. Arthur looked over Mark's shoulder, watching him finish off that last of one of his knights.

"My goodness, Mr. Malone! You're an excellent artist! You got it better than he looks!"

Arthur's compliment brought back something that Mark hadn't felt in a long time. There was appreciation in the driver's voice that caught Mark off guard. He smiled, a real smile this time, not one that he usually pushed out at the last minute.

After Union Station closed, Arthur took Mr. Malone back to the hotel, Mark packing all the little items he purchased in his packing boxes along with his clothes. He picked up the clothes he had worn the night before and was going to throw them in the laundry hamper, when something fell out from his jacket pocket. He looked down at it and picked it up. It was the envelope that Ronald had given him. He threw the clothes in the hamper and turned the lamp on by his bed, sitting down. He opened it. There was a letter and, inside, was a business card. He read the letter:

Dear Mr. Malone,

I know how you like to do things a little different than others, so here's someone you might want to see while you're in D.C. I hope you fit in. I've been there when I was younger and kept in touch. Watch what you do and say. These people are for real.

Your friend and driver,

Ronald Schellinger

The business card was for a fortuneteller, not far from Mark's hotel. All it said was her name and address. He turned the card over. On the back, there was a hand-written 32 scribbled in ink. He turned the card back over and examined it a little longer, placing the card in his wallet. He called the front desk.

"Yes, could you get my driver ready? I have one more place to go tonight."

It was about midnight when the limo pulled up, parking on the side of the road. Arthur opened the door, letting Mark out, who was nervous as ever. He looked up the small, stone walkway that led up to the house on the business card. Mark looked at Arthur, who was looking at the house, watching for any movement in the windows.

"Are you sure this is where you want to go, Mr. Malone?" Arthur walked back to the limo, looking back every-so-often, waiting for Mark to turn and get back into the limo.

But he didn't.

Holding onto the card, he made his way up the steps and onto the porch, looking for the doorbell. The whole porch was draped in darkness, no light or candles burning anywhere. Mark found the door and knocked on it several times, waiting for an answer. The door opened.

An old woman, probably in her seventies, stuck her head out, looking up at Mark's face, and then down at the card. She was dressed in a silky gown covered with sequins and copper pieces hanging off of it in some sort of design. She took the card and turned it over, smiling when she saw the number on the back. She let Mark in, her voice echoing through the dark house.

"So, you know Ronald? What is he up to these days?" Before Mark had a chance to answer she laughed, shaking her head.

"Driving limousines? I don't believe it. I always thought he would do something more with his life. I read his future and it was different, but he didn't follow that path. He should have. He would've been a lot happier than he is now. The way it seems, he's only going to live a few more years. He's too old for driving. He needs his rest." She had read Mark's mind.

Madame Coudiva somehow opened up his mind and read what he had been thinking out loud. She looked at him then, smiling, knowing that he was truly believing her now.

Before, when he had walked up the stairs, doubts about her ability played through his mind, with fake crystal balls and fake promises and dreams. But he looked at her, face cast in shadows by the many candles that lit the room they were walking in, and knew that she was the genuine article.

The room was small but comfortable. He saw the crystal ball, sitting on a black oak mount, filled with a milky white substance. The substance swirled to life when Madame Coudiva approached and sat down in front of it. She motioned for Mark to sit on the other side. He did, watching the substance reach for him inside the ball, as if it had hands. He shook his head in astonishment, his hands beginning to sweat.

He watched the Madame slip the card in her pocket and reach for the crystal ball, it reaching for her in return. Mark was mesmerized by the swirling of the mist inside and how the gypsy could follow the pattern with her hands above the ball, not even touching it. Then, unexpectedly, an image appeared. It was Mark, with a woman, and they were in bed together. The old gypsy chuckled.

"You are very active in the art of love-making, are you not?" She didn't want him to answer. She kept going, the mist swirling a little faster. She changed the scenery with a movement of her hands. It was Mark again, with a woman, but it was in focus, closer than before. It was Jessica with him. She was on top of him, her face close to the crystal ball. She called out his name. He could see the words on her lips but couldn't hear them. He watched closer.

Jessica was moving faster, kissing him while she moaned and heaved on top, when someone came in out of the background. It was a man. He was a younger man, about 10 years younger than Mark, and he had something in his hand, a stick or bat shaped object. He swung it at Jessica, knocking her over, then at Mark, pummeling him blow after blow. The Mark in the crystal ball was bloody, almost dead, reaching out for Jessica. But she didn't move.

Mark reached out to the crystal ball, looking at Madame Coudiva. She let the mist fade and turned her gaze to him.

"She dies that night. You take her to the hospital, suffering broken bones yourself, but she doesn't make it. She has internal bleeding. The other man is burning with hatred for you. He never liked you; never will. Unless you do something to turn his anger away, she will die. You must be wary of these futures, for you have also been hurt. You cannot look into your wife's eyes ever again. She knows the truth about you and Jessica. She had doubts but the truth is finally revealed. You are out in the street, fighting for a hold on life, with a crippled hand and a disfigured face. You never find out who the man is that killed her. You life is never the same. Is it worth it, Mr. Malone?"

Mark shook his head.

What has this come to? Is that was Jessica has been calling for? Is there someone after her, a boyfriend, fiancée waiting for her to do something so he can kill her? Mark had to call her.

She has to be in danger. He looked at the gypsy and gave her a handful of bills out of his wallet. She accepted and waits for any questions.

"Can I change this future myself, now that I know what is to happen?" She nods but doesn't think that as a good alternative to solving what the crystal ball has shown them.

"Forget this woman now, before you get yourself in too deep!" Mark forces a smile and leaves then, watching her out the limo window, her shadow disappearing from the window in her house.

I have to do something, no matter what Madame Coudiva says.

The night goes by and he sleeps, dreaming of Jessica, dreaming the same fate that was in the crystal ball. He wakes several times during the night, sweating profusely, looking around to see only darkness and the shadows in the hotel room. He lies back down to sleep.

The phone wakes him up. It's about 8:45 in the morning. It's the same young man at the desk downstairs with the squeaky voice, scratchily telling Mark that he has a phone call. Mark hears Jessica's voice on the other end.

"Well, are you ready yet?" Mark can hear a hint of excitement in her voice coming out in her immediate question.

What am I to say? He thought before saying anything, trying to come up with some good excuse to tell her. She knew what he was planning.

"Don't tell me you're canceling, Mark! You already said you'd take me out and we'd go somewhere. Besides, I really need to talk to you." He couldn't stay away from her. There was just something that attracted him to her, to Jessica, the sweetest woman he had ever met and probably ever will.

"Fine. Give me your address and I'll be there in an hour with my limo, okay?" He could almost hear her smile as he wrote down the address on a scratchpad on the desk next to him, talking for another couple of minutes then setting the receiver down, only to

pick it back up again. He called the front desk.

"Ready my driver."

Chapter Eight

- AGAINST BETTER JUDGMENT -

Mark was there in an hour, sitting in the back of the limo, watching as the Green Maple subdivision came into view. It was a beautiful place for homes in D.C., with groomed trees and flowers that lined the sidewalks to the doors. Each home had a two-car garage linked to it in some way; if not from the side then built in under the home on a hill above the others. Jessica lived in one that rested on a hill, far above anyone else's. The streets wound around each other and connected in various ways, Mark watching Arthur's face turn red as he circled the same street for the third time.

When they finally got to Jessica's home, Mark saw her in the front window of her house. She stared for a long time out at the limo then finally came out, locking the door behind her. She set the alarm.

She was just as beautiful as ever.

Her hair was still long and flowing, her big brown eyes staring at Mark, her little nose planted between those perfect eyes. She wore a conservative woman's blue business suit and carried a briefcase with her to the limo. Arthur offered to take the briefcase. She gave it to him gladly and made her way into the limo, sitting across from Mark. When Arthur began to drive away, Jessica reached over to Mark and gave him a hug.

She smelled wonderful.

Her face was soft and warm, just like he remembered it. She sat back down. Jessica spoke first.

"So, are we still on for Dargini's?" He smiled and nodded.

"We still have reservations. Why? Is there something important you need to do that I don't know about?" He signaled with his hand to the briefcase up front that sat with Arthur. She tried to smile but, for some reason, couldn't. Something was wrong.

"I called you for a reason, Mark. Something's happened. I don't know how to tell you this." She stopped. He could tell it was important. She never had trouble telling him anything before. They were always truthful about things to each other. It began to eat at Mark's patience. He put his hand on hers, comforting her as best he could.

"Just tell me whenever you're ready. I'll understand. It's me, Mark; your good friend. Nothing can be that bad." Jessica smiled this time, a nice one that made Mark remember why he had been so attracted to her.

She began to relax a little more after they got to Dargini's, feasting on the finest Italian food in the D.C. area, her thoughts seeming to linger a bit when they talked about years gone by. It seemed as if everything was fine. They laughed and talked for over an hour, sipping on wine and dabbling into previous conversation as they had in the limo. It related back to what was in the briefcase.

She was silent for a time and then spoke to him, as if every word for her was hard to get out. Jessica asked Mark if she could get the briefcase and Mark had Arthur bring it to her, Arthur walking away quickly so as not to disturb them. She sat it in her lap and opened it, pulling out a manila envelope. She handed it to Mark.

"This is for you. I can't find any way to tell you so I'll just let you see for yourself." Mark took the envelope and broke the seal on it, opening it, all the while watching Jessica's face.

She was hiding her emotions. He could tell she wanted to say something. Mark pulled out the contents of the envelope.

There were pictures; pictures of Denise with another man...pictures of Denise with many other men. And the dates of the pictures were on them also; dating back since Mark and Denise were first married. He looked them over several times, looking closely at Denise's face on everyone. Mark knew that she probably had another man but this put him in total shock. He looked up at Jessica.

"How'd you get these?" She reached in her briefcase again and pulled out a letter. It was a printout of a detective's resume.

"I hired Emmett to be Denise's limo driver throughout her times at different sets on movies. He stayed with her and she began to like him as a friend and hired him herself. I couldn't bear to see you with a person that made you unhappy. Mark, she made you miserable. She's no good."

Mark was a little upset at the idea of Jessica prying into his life.

"What makes you think I was unhappy with Denise?"

"I know, I saw the pictures of you in the papers with her. She just used you. I would never do that. I was hurt after I left from college. I couldn't imagine you with anybody else but me after that day in high school. Mark, I love you." Mark was stunned.

He slid the pictures back into the envelope and sat them to the side. He didn't know what to say.

"What do you want me to say? Do you want me to leave her? Is that was this is?" His guess was right. Jessica didn't say anything.

She closed her briefcase and sat it by her chair. She reached for his hands and took them in hers.

"Mark, I know this is confusing, but I want you back. I don't care if you're still married to Denise. You have enough evidence right now to divorce her and get half of everything. But that doesn't matter. All I care about is you. I need you Mark. I spent all of my years in college thinking about you and what our lives would be like if we were together. Mark, we would be happy. I know we would."

Mark didn't let go of her hands. He held them tighter. How he wanted to be with her. Those times were the best for him. He had always loved her more than anyone else. But what could he do? He wasn't about to make her another one on his list. He had come here on an escapade, yes, but he didn't want to make her one of his beds. She could see the doubt on his face.

"Mark, let's get out of here and go back to my place. There, we can talk about this without any disturbances." He saw something on her face. He remembered the look she had that day when she came into his room wearing just her graduation robe. That same look passed over her face right now. He walked back with her to the limo.

There was an air of silence about them as they walked and Arthur could sense it as they approached the limo.   But the chauffeur said nothing, probably because he knew it was none of his business. Mark handed the manila envelope to Arthur and pulled out a card from his wallet. It was his lawyer's name and fax #. He gave it to Arthur. Arthur nodded in understanding. His driver sat the envelope in the front seat with him and slid the card into his pocket, holding the door until both Jessica and Mark were inside.

Mark really had no choice. He had the evidence and Jessica was right; this was his chance. If he didn't take it right now, he would never get away and would remain unhappy.

But what was going to happen? How would he explain seeing his old girlfriend again and what if it was all just a set up? What then? So many things ran through Mark's mind as they drove back to Jessica's house. But Mark refused to let things worry him. He had gotten this far on his instincts; he should just keep on relying on them.

They drove back to Jessica's house; Mark letting Arthur off duty until he needed him, which he really didn't know would be again. Everything seemed so confusing right now.

One day, Mark was enjoying his life and, the next, his world suddenly became confusing. He looked over at Jessica, who seemed to know where he was at right now.

"Mark, everything will be okay. I promise."

Arthur drove away in the limo and Mark followed Jessica up to her house on the hill. In moments, they were in Jessica's house. She locked the door behind them and set the security alarm behind them. Jessica sat her briefcase down.

Her home was beautiful. Most of the walls were filled with paintings, a lot of his paintings, and a few other painters that he knew, mostly friends or acquaintances, a few even he was a fan of. The walls were a beige putty-like substance, almost a Mexican style home, complete with a spiral staircase going upstairs.

Jessica had taken off the jacket to her business suit earlier when they arrived, now only clothed in a long sleeve, white business shirt and skirt. Jessica began unbuttoning each button, showing Mark the curves of her breasts. She slid her skirt off, showing her shapely hips, then stepped out of the skirt, her panties peeking out from under the long shirt. She untied her hair and let it fall about her shoulders.

"I want you, Mark. I don't want you to leave here until you know how much I care."

She closed in on him, her nails scratching over his shirt, in seconds under his shirt, digging softly into his skin. She breathed on his neck, her face close to his, her nipples hard against his chest. He wanted to hold her and he began to reach out, his lips on her, his hands rubbing against her bare thighs.

Then the vision came into his mind. The vision the fortuneteller had read in the crystal ball. Mark could see Jessica's bruised face, bloody and red. He pulled away.

Jessica came back to him, her eyes staring hard, her hands rubbing harder, nails scratching at his back more intense than before.

"Mark, what's wrong?" The vision was stronger this time, Madame Coudiva's voice echoing Jessica's fate into his mind, over and over.

The woman will die, the woman will die; internal bleeding, internal bleeding.

"What are we doing here, Jessica? You contact me and tell me that you've been having my wife spied on for years, that you love me, and you just expect me to accept it and have sex with you? What kind of man do you think I am?"

He felt her hands reach for the button to his pants and they were off in moments, Mark stepping out of them and closer to his love. Mark was helpless against her. Soon, the visions were gone from his mind, replaced by Jessica's face.

She moaned as she moved against him, both lying on her sofa in the living room, bodies sweating and eager. She squeezed him tighter. He was blown over with passion, taken aback by the love she felt for him. Hours went by and they made love, room after room; in the shower, on the floor in front of the fireplace, out on the balcony overlooking the rest of the Green Maple residents.

The night came soon and Jessica was asleep in Mark's arms, her body warm against his. They lay in her plush bedroom. That's where they had finished their sexcapades. Mark was unable to sleep. He kept staring at the bedroom door.

Any moment, he thought. Any moment someone's going to come in through that door and beat us with a bat. He was tense. Now even more so since Jessica had told him the way she felt about him. He looked down at her face, her beautiful face, rubbing his fingers down her cheek to her chin. He lifted her head up slowly and kissed her lips. She moaned in her sleep and snuggled closer to him. He sunk down into the bed, nestled with Jessica, his eyes dropping shut. Sleep finally overtook him.

He awoke to the creak of a door. He heard someone putting in the alarm code downstairs but was still groggy and half asleep. Now, he heard someone at the stairway downstairs. Jessica awoke, too, sitting up in the bed. She looked over at Mark fearfully and slid out of bed. She motioned for Mark to get out of bed, too. She whispered to him.

"Mark, you have to hide! Please, for your own safety! Hide!"

Hide, Mark thought. What the hell? He whispered back to her.

"Is this some kind of joke? Who's downstairs that I can't see?"

Wrong question. He wished he had never asked that. The answer came as she scooted him into the closet by the bed, shutting the door behind him.

"My husband."

Husband! Oh fuck! Mark put his head in his hands. *What have I gotten myself into now?*

Husband! I can't believe this! He lifted his head up just in time to see a man enter into the bedroom. Mark hunched down quietly as he watched the two converse.

"Hi, honey. I didn't expect you home so soon. Get off early?" Jessica asked her husband, covering herself with a bathrobe. Her husband smiled at her and came closer, grabbing her by the waist.

"I couldn't wait to get home, if you know what I mean!" He smiled at her, reaching inside her robe. He pulled out her breasts and began sucking on them. He was a short man but very muscular and strong, picking Jessica up off the floor with ease and laid her on the bed.

He started on her immediately, moving fast, his moans louder than hers. His name was Clark, Mark found out from Jessica's moans, and he didn't seem to satisfy her. He leaned his head back and, with one quick push, collapsed on her before she even had time to finish. At that time, Mark had a good look at his face.

It was the man in the vision. Clark was the guy that had caught them together. But how would that happen? He hadn't caught them at all.

Jessica was looking over at Mark in the closet while Clark began kissing on her again, moving down under the sheets. She closed her eyes and wiggled when Clark hit a sensitive spot with his tongue. She opened her eyes back up and looked at Mark in his hiding place, waving at him while Clark couldn't see. Then her husband drove her wild beneath the sheets. She moaned.

"Oh, Mark! That feels so good! Mark, please don't stop!" Clark stopped instantly and came up from under the sheets.

"Who did you call me, Jess?" She smiled at him. Mark almost had a heart attack.

She was doing this on purpose! She didn't accidentally say his name. She was up to something.

"I said Mark, Clark honey. Why, don't you like me screaming my other lover's name?" *She was pushing it.*

Clark smiled. He was chuckling now.

He thought it was a joke! He went back under the covers and started all over again. She did the same thing. Mark's name was called out several times. Mark sat in the closet, watching Clark bang away at Jessica with great strength. But Mark knew all her moans were false. He knew what her moans sounded like. Clark was too inadequate to please her. After a while, Jessica just laid there, letting him finish off again and collapse. Soon, he left to take a shower.

She rushed to the closet and pulled Mark back onto the bed, Mark scrambling to make for the door with his clothes. Jessica grabbed at him, her naked skin pressed against his own.

"Please don't leave! Not yet." She pulled him to the bed and climbed back onto him. Already, Mark had a pretty strong erection from watching the two of them. She pushed him into her and began rocking back and forth lightly.

Mark could hear the shower going in the next room, Clark talking to his wife as she sat on top of Mark. Jessica answered with yes and no mostly, feeling another orgasm build up within her. She moaned a little and held Mark down on the bed, not letting him up. He tried to push her off but she held him down just long enough for Clark to walk back in. She was in the middle of orgasm, moaning at the top of her lungs, when Clark walked in, a towel around his waist. His mouth fell open. Jessica smiled.

"Look, honey, I'm fucking another man! Do you like watching me fuck other men? Oh god, yes!" Jessica dropped onto Mark's chest, out of breath, shaking from her orgasm. She held onto him tightly, convulsing with each pulse of pleasure. She looked back up at her husband.

"Do you like this Mark? My husband and I do this all the time. Don't we honey?" Mark looked over at Jessica's husband, Clark, who was now smiling and walking closer.

He dropped his towel.

Chapter 9

- DOCTOR'S ORDERS -

Mark was far beyond gone. What had he gotten himself into? What else could happen? Jessica was on him, still out of breath from the last orgasm, sliding underneath the black sheets, her sweaty skin sticking to him, taking even longer for her to wait and watch.

Watch, Mark thought, noticing Clark walking closer to him and not his wife. There had been days when Mark had given in to things he didn't want to do but this was definitely not one of them. He began to get out of bed. Clark, watching Mark getting jittery, held his manhood out to him.

"Take it, Mark. Try it on for size. It's not so bad once you start. You get used to it after a while." He stood at the edge of the bed now, waiting for Mark to grab hold. Mark stood up on the bed, a pillow in front of his own crotch.

Jessica looked confused.

"What's wrong, Mark? Come on, give it a try. I love to watch two men go at it." Mark hopped off the bed and grabbed his clothes from under the bed where Jessica had hid them when Clark had come in earlier.

"Fuck this! What the hell's gotten into you, Jessica? I thought you were different than everyone else. I thought you cared." He glanced at Clark when he said that. For some reason, that last sentence had flowed out with more care than he had wished to give it while being naked and vulnerable in front of her husband. Clark looked over at Jessica. He was angry.

"Yeah? What is this shit, Jess? Are you going for this guy or what? You just told me he'd be into this, that's all. Are you fucking telling me you have feelings for this shit?" Mark could sense the anger in his voice. Clark had apparently gone unaware that Jessica did have something, or so Mark thought, for him.

Mark backed away and slid his underwear on, standing for moments longer, struggling on what he should do. Had she changed that much in the time they had spent apart? Was he only here for pleasure and no real love? Did he even need to get into this argument? In no time, Clark was on her, smacking at her hands that covered her face.

"Stupid bitch! I can't believe you! I thought we had an understanding! And you . . ....", he stopped smacking at her, pointing at Mark. Clark moved away from Jessica and reached underneath the bed, his hands pulling out something.

It was a fucking bat. Something had told Mark that this would happen. It was all too good to be true.

"I'm going to bat you to the fucking head!"

Madame Coudiva was right after all. Mark lunged. Clark was caught off guard. Mark's right shoulder slammed into Clark's diaphragm, knocking the wind out of him, sending him reeling to the floor, his hand with the bat caught in between the bedpost and the nightstand. Mark yanked the bat from his hand and threw it to the side, putting his foot on Clark's chest to hold him at bay.

"Are you alright, Jessica? Jessica?" He looked over on the bed at Jessica.

Gone. She wasn't on the bed any longer. He turned and saw the bat as it came in contact with the side of his head. Mark flew off balance and felt his body spin out of control. He hit the bed, the room spinning around him, voices the only thing he could concentrate on without the pounding in his head getting worse. He could hear Jessica's voice first.

"Tie him up! I can't believe this! Stupid ass! How could you let him get the bat? Do you know what he could've done if he wanted? I can't believe you stood there like that while he tackled you. You better be glad he's a shoe-in for a pretty face."

Then came Clark's voice. He was standing beside the bed now, off the floor, his voice biting and sharp.

"I'll go get the rope. Watch him while I'm gone. I want to have some fun with this one. I'll call the others, too. This is going to be a long night. I guess I'll make some coffee while I'm downstairs." Clark chuckled.

Call the others, Mark thought, realizing that he was in what seemed to be the deepest and darkest pit of trouble he could ever fathom.

Whatever was happening tonight could not be good, he concluded, trying to raise himself on the bed.

He heard Jessica's voice again, a little closer this time.

"I'll use the handcuffs till you get back." Then her voice was just a whisper in Mark's direction.

"Take all the time you need. I want him to myself for a couple." She bent over and began searching for something underneath the bed. It rang out a metallic clang when she picked it up. She laid it on the bed next to Mark. Jessica flipped him over, her naked body climbing on top of him. She handcuffed his right hand, and then his left, holding the bat with one hand, then went to his ankles, connecting them to the rails with another pair of cuffs. Soon, Mark couldn't move. He was naked, spread eagle on the bed, his pillow used for cover now on the floor. Jessica moved over him.

"Mark. Mark, honey, are you alright? I'm sorry I had to do that, but you were ruining my plan. I want you to hear what I have to say before everyone gets here."

Jessica sat her naked ass on him. He could feel her moistness dripping on him in anticipation as well as what had gone on earlier.

"I'm not the little princess you once knew. Clark's introduced me to a new crowd, a livelier bunch than I've ever known. They like to try new things. They're going to try new things on you, too, dear heart. I just wanted you to know that." She smiled and leaned down next to Mark's ear, licking his lobe with her tongue.

"But I want you to know that I did enjoy making love to you. I miss that about my life, making love; but not enough to change." She grabbed his cock in her hands. It was still semi-erect and it seemed to respond to her assertiveness, stiffening in her hand.

"You have a hard cock. It's going to get used a lot tonight. I hope you're ready. A lot of people will be watching tonight, so don't you fail me. It will make Clark very angry and, I think you know how he gets when he's angry." She touched the bat to Mark's skin. The metal was cold and it made him jerk in surprise. Jessica giggled.

"God, it's going to be so fun to see you with all my friends tonight. I want to give you something first, you know, to get you ready for what's ahead." Jessica let go of the bat and let it roll off the bed. It clanged on the floor, rolling back and forth until it finally stopped.

Mark's eyesight was still fuzzy and he couldn't see that well, but he could feel Jessica slide her way down to his groin. She hovered over his manhood, her hands cold and alive, stroking, tugging, her mouth eagerly taking in his wholeness. For some reason, and he didn't know why, this moment, this feeling inside him, excited him greatly. He was scared to death but, at the same time, he felt a rush of adrenaline as Jessica's mouth pumped vigorously up and down on his cock.

He was about to come when he heard footsteps and Clark's voice erupted.

"What the fuck are you doing? Are you crazy?" Mark felt Jessica's mouth release him and there was a loud smack. Jessica fell off the bed. Clark walked closer, his voice still as biting as it was before he left.

"I can't fucking believe you! You're getting ready to make this guy come and we've got friends coming over to see him? Can't you at least wait until they get here?" Clark had apparently retrieved the rope from downstairs and now knotted a few good knots around Mark's hands and arms, uncuffing the cuffs, hog-tying his captive on the bed in moments.

They must have done this before, Mark thought. It was several minutes before anyone did anything to him again.

They were wandering around the room; one watching him while the other went downstairs, standing in the corner, sometimes sitting on the bed next to him. Then he felt Jessica's hands on him again. It was to gag him. There was a sock in his mouth, and then something tied around his head to hold it in. Mark gagged several times then gradually became accustomed to it as Jessica was finishing off her other duties.

There was a blindfold and a leash, along with some skintight pants that were crotch less, sort of like leggings, her fingers pulling them on while Clark went back downstairs.

Jessica slid onto the bed next to Mark. She grabbed at his cock between his legs, slowly sliding her hand up and down his shaft, her lips touching his bruised face. She leaned down and put his cock in her mouth several times but never started as she did before, apparently saving him now for the others.

"I get you last, after everyone else has you. I hope you can hold out for the good stuff until then or I'll have to punish you. Oh, but I think you'll like that." Jessica put his cock in her mouth again and began to hum. It brought back that same sensation he had earlier, fear and excitement mixed. She was trying her hardest to get him to come.

But why? She let go of Mark and began speaking to him, her voice now deep and filled with lust. She told him things.

"I want you so bad right now, Mark. It's not fair that I don't get you first. I brought you here. Maybe I can ask Clark again. Maybe he'll let me." She seemed sad and disappointed.

She was definitely not in control of the situation.

The downstairs door opened and shut.

Oh shit, they were here. Mark heard footsteps and heard several male voices. One of them was Clarks.

"Here, I'll get this side, you get the other side. We'll lift on three. One. . Two. . Three." Mark was lifted off the bed as two men hefted him down the stairs, hog-tied, to what he thought was the living room. He heard several people laughing and giggling, male and female, and the air was cold, extremely cold. He could hear the air conditioner going. Clark and the other man sat Mark on a table and left him there for a couple of moments. Mark couldn't see but could smell wine and food, like they were serving dinner and he was sitting in on it. Mark sat there, naked, waiting for someone to do something. Now this made him edgy. His head had cleared from the bat swing and he heard someone come close.

It was another woman. He could tell by her touch. She was strong but soft, her hands untying the gag and pulling out the sock in between his lips. She held something out to him, let it touch his lips.

It was cheese; the fine cheese that they served at parties. The woman let him eat then leaned down, her lips rubbing against his own, her lipstick thick on his dry lips. She then offered a glass to his lips. He drank. It was great wine. She laughed and leaned down to wipe the wine off his lips with hers and spoke.

"You're mine first." Suddenly, he smelled a rich, deep hospital smell, as if someone had put it in a bottle and opened it right in front of his nostrils.

Oh shit, Mark thought, knowing for some reason that it was about to get a little more hairy than he wanted. There was a sharp pain in his right arm and then it was gone, the needle pulling out, leaving an aching feeling for moments only. Then the drugs took hold.

It was like someone trying to shake you from sleep but you just couldn't wake up.

It felt so good. The voices were muddled, the laughs bright and vocal.

As they untied the ropes, Mark did not fight. Mark couldn't fight. His arms were heavy, his legs aching. All he wanted to do was stretch out. Things were spinning even worse than they were when the bat had struck him. The drugs flowed through his veins, his limbs on fire. Clark's voice broke through the drugs. It was muddled also, but he could tell by the deepness of it that it was Jessica's husband.

"Folks, I'd like to introduce you to tonight's entertainment; Mark Malone. Mr. Malone, would you please raise your hand and say hello to the ladies and gents gracing our presence tonight." Mark tried to raise his hand but it was too heavy. He closed his eyes. They all laughed. He laughed with them. Everything was funny. Then they got quiet. He felt someone approaching. Then there was something warm on him; and it was wet.

Unknown hands untied the blindfold from his eyes.

Mark opened his eyes. There was a woman; red, flaming hair that cascaded down her back, sitting on top of him, naked. Her long hair brushed against his bare chest as she leaned forward. Deep, blue eyes penetrated through the drugs and he could see her now through his lust-filled eyes. She had his cock in her hands, pushing it inside of her. He almost died from the pleasure when his cock slid into her.

It feels so incredible! This must have been the woman feeding him earlier.

She was stronger than he had thought. She pumped up and down on him, slow at first, then moved into deep, hard strokes, her moans directed out to the others, as if her and Mark were the show in a play of sorts. It felt like he could fuck for hours, letting her ride. Then Jessica was there, hovering next to him while the redhead moved, a smile on her face as well. She spoke.

"Do you like that, Mark? I can see that you do. You don't have to answer. Just remember to save some for me, alright?" Mark nodded, or what he thought a nod was, only to get an echo of laughter from all that stood around him. There must have been at least twelve other people standing, all naked, watching his face, the red-head's face, watching her spill her juices all over Mark's thighs then grab onto his cock.

Mark could feel it erupt. It felt like a volcano at the last minute, exploding out into the open for the whole world to see. He let out a moan, the people spinning fast around him. It felt as if the whole world shook on the tip of his erection. He smiled now, seeing the redhead to the side of him with the others that stood, smiling; her body wet and dripping. She tilted her head up and motioned for him to look.

At what, Mark thought, watching as another woman climbed on top of him, licking off the previous juices, squeezing his cock between her legs. She had the needle in her hand also, waving it in front of him.

She was gorgeous. This woman was in her early twenties; she had short, black hair that came just above her shoulders and a little upturned nose that fit perfectly in between those milky dark brown eyes that stared out at him. She had small, petite breasts that perked out on her chest, like a young girls, just reaching maturity. He wanted to reach out, to put those nipples in his mouth himself, but he couldn't.

Something was holding him down. He looked around. They had him tied down with Velcro straps. He looked back up.

Ouch; the pain again. The woman on top handed the needle to another and began going down on Mark, her hands rubbing against his sweaty body. He looked down at her, chin on his chest, following her eyes. She stared at him while she pleased him, her mouth sucking hard as she sipped the remainder of the juices from inside him, her fingers slick with orgasm and sweat. She laid her body on top of his, sliding up to his face, her perk nipples rubbing against his chest, her mouth on his. She spoke in between his lips, her breath pushing into his mouth, something a woman had never done to him. This drove Mark wild. He wanted this woman so bad. He needed her.

"What do you want, Mark? Is there something you want Claudia to do for you? Is there something that you need?" She reached down his chest and let her nails drag against his skin, sending shivers down through to his toes. He answered her.

"I want your breasts in my mouth." The woman was almost shocked. She didn't expect him to answer, let alone request specifics. She didn't have big breasts but what she did have was soon hovering just over his face, close to his mouth, a nipple rubbing against his lips. She got off on teasing him. What seemed like minutes turned into an hour, Claudia sliding Mark gently inside while she rubbed her chest against his face. He was about to burst again. He could feel it. Claudia could tell, too. Mark became stiff inside of her and he closed his eyes. She slid off him, backing away from his erect penis and the pleasure it held for him. This was more torture than Mark could bear. She stood by several others, men and women, a seductive smile still etched on her face. Her voice was far now, back away from the table.

"I'm done, Mr. Malone. It's time for someone else to give you a try." He looked around. His manhood was throbbing, raging for someone else to stab in to. He saw Jessica in the crowd, her body oiled down, shiny from the chandelier in the kitchen, just a room away. She approached him.

"You need to watch this, Mark. This is something you don't see everyday." She climbed on top of him and almost mounted him. He urged her to, raising his mid-section, almost sliding inside her on his own. But she rose above him, her tight ass high in the air. Then a man approached, climbing onto the table behind her, his manhood out, wearing the same leather leggings on that Mark had.   He mounted Jessica from behind and began ramming away. That drove Mark crazy. He was beyond hard, rock solid, waiting for someone, anyone, yet watching Jessica take another cock inside her, seeing her face and realizing that it wasn't him giving her the pleasure. He pleaded with her.

"Please let me have you! I am almost there. Just a little bit. Please, Jessica!" But she was in pleasureville, population just her, feeling the man behind her pound away. Mark could feel drips of her wetness all over him from the two of them, feeling Jessica's hands on his shoulders, feel her legs slide up against his hips as she took every thrust by the man behind her, every urgent stroke with a moan of pleasure. Then the man behind her came. He let out a moan and kept his cock inside of her, letting it explode within, Jessica's body shaking from pleasure.

The man pulled out and climbed off the table. Jessica collapsed, body sliding over Mark's, her face next to his, breathing hard, her body still shaking from the last orgasm.

Jessica climbed off slowly and the group continued for what seemed a full day, one taking a turn with Mark, others having sex right on top of him for him to see, for him to taste, for him to feel the explosions, to see everyone in pleasure.

There were two more needle pricks. Mark was in such a haze that he didn't know where he was after awhile; didn't know whom he was

with; couldn't see a foot in front of him. He just let things happen.
After that, he let consciousness go, let it slip away from his control.
Mark couldn't remember much after that. All had felt like a dream; a
strange dream in which you don't try to decipher, just accept it as
that; a dream.

Chapter 10

- RECOVERY ROOM -

It all seemed so hazy and dreamlike when the sun came shining in through the windows early that morning. Mark didn't question where he was; he knew. He could tell by the scent of the plush interior that it was the limo and that Arthur, by some alternative means, had come to get him this morning. The world around the limo rushed by, making Mark's head spin even more as Arthur pulled the limo out of Jessica's subdivision.

"Oh shit! I feel terrible!" He leaned over and lay back down on the padded seats, his body aching with every movement. Mark managed to lean over and click the intercom button.

"Yes, Mr. Malone?" Arthur's voice piped up. It was cheery but there was a hint of concern in it as they drove back to the hotel, the older man looking back at his client every-so-often.

"What happened?" That was all Mark could get out. The needles from last night, whatever they carried, still had a hold on him and his body was fighting against it. So far, his body was losing; losing badly. Each limb, each joint, everything that had a nerve, ached. Mark just lay there and let himself sweat it out while Arthur told him the details of this morning.

"First, Mr. Malone, I could have sworn that you were working for her, but, after what I saw this morning, I think a little differently now. Since you didn't call last night, I went ahead and assumed that you had been invited to stay the night and were going to call me in the morning. But your Mrs. Friend called me this morning, about 6:00 a.m. and said that you weren't feeling well and that you partied a little too hard last night. When I got at her residence, there were at least five or six cars parked outside her house. Partied too hard, indeed, you're not even wearing the same clothes you had on yesterday."

Arthur chuckled a little at the end of his sentence, watching as Mark looked down at his clothes.

These were Clark's clothes, the ones he had on from last night. Someone else must have dressed me last night. He could feel the effects of the drug inside him take hold again and he slid back into a corner of the limo, eyes burning, his fingertips alive and on fire. A look of concern crossed Arthur's face.

"Are you okay, sir? Do you need me to take you to a doctor? I know where a good one is." Mark sat up, his eyes watering. A feeling of nausea began to overcome him. He brushed it off the best he could.

"I'll be just fine. I just need to get to my room at the hotel and take a long cool shower. That sounds good, doesn't it? A cool shower." Mark's voice slurred. He hadn't felt this out of it since college when he went to those frat parties all those years ago. It almost felt good except for the fact that it didn't seem to go away at all by the time they got to the hotel.

His legs still ached, his fingers were still numb, and on top of that he had to get out and walk. The limo slowed down in front of the plaza hotel, Arthur sliding out of the front seat and hurrying around the limousine. Mark looked up as Arthur opened the back door to help him stand up. The older man wrapped a jacket that he got from out of the trunk around Mark and whistled to the bellboy for a wheelchair. Mark could hear the bellboy wheel the chair over and felt himself plop down into it, but everything was blurry. It seemed that, when he stood up, it increased the effects of the drug to his legs and made them go completely numb, feeling an awful lot like putty. He heard the bellboy's voice.

"Gee, Mister, what's wrong with him?"

Arthur was a quick thinker, all right.

"Dental surgery. He's still feeling the anesthesia. It'll take a while to wear off."

Good comeback, Mark thought, or so he hoped. All thought process was out of the question. Everything felt cool to the touch now. Instead of the intense heat and numbness earlier, he now felt everything, almost like last night.

He could hear the champagne glasses, the laughing, giggling noises the women around him made. Then he remembered their faces, their slippery bodies on top of him. He started to dream about that. Everything that happened last night felt so real. It might have actually appealed to him more if he wasn't pushed into it so quick.

The air wafted by his face. Voices, still figures moving past, that's all Mark saw as Arthur pushed him through the hallways and into the nearby elevator. It almost put him to sleep. Arthur nudged him with a finger.

"Stay awake, Mr. Malone, you're almost to your room. Talk to me. Or at least nod your head or something to let me know that you're coherent."

Mark nodded to each ring that the elevator made as it touched a floor and went by. He still remembered that he was on the 9th floor of the building and that is was paradise inside. After that, train of thought went back to the women and the drugs. How it made him feel was almost dreamlike, like in a still moment in time able to move and feel in control of everything. Arthur patted him on the shoulder, jarring him to consciousness slightly.

"Yes, here were are." He felt Arthur's hands in his pockets as he searched for the keys. The door unlocked. Mark's eyes were completely closed. The room was quiet and there were no lights on as he was rolled in. Arthur wheeled him hurriedly to the bathroom and helped him into the shower, leaning him against the wall with his left hand as he turned on the shower with his right. Mark objected.

"Hey, what about my clothes? Aren't you going to help me get them off first?" Arthur retorted with a couple of words.

"Those aren't your clothes." The shower water was freezing. It hit him like millions of tiny icicles.

Ice cold and full of coffee.

At least, that's what it felt like to Mark. Every cell in his body jerked awake, his hands reaching out for the nozzle, spraying it directly into his face. It felt like he could drown himself and it would actually feel good. Mark stood there for a long time, feeling the water soak through the clothes he had on, his legs waking back up. He could feel his fingers again and his eyes slowly opened. It was still dark, except for one light on outside the bathroom. He could see Arthur there, standing in the doorway, waiting for some sign of betterment. Mark smiled at him. Arthur chuckled and handed him a towel.

The day was over. The night was, too. Mark made it over to his bed before dismissing Arthur and slept well over 12 hours, his body pushing the last of the drugs out of his system. Arthur was gone now, probably waiting for the next drama for Mark to put him through. Mark's mind had finally cleared and he could think. A whole day had gone by and the first thing that leaped into his mind was Jessica, that poor girl.

What the hell had she gotten herself into? What a change she had gone through since they had last seen each other. Holy shit! Whatever had happened, it had to start with that Clark fellow. He was a shady character if Mark ever did see one. Years and years of waiting, wanting, dreaming, and the girl of my dreams turned out to be a freak!

Oh well, it was over now. At least Mark was safe from whatever activities she was doing. He pulled his arm out from under the covers. It still ached from that night, though. Whatever they had given him that had kept him shaken well into the next day. The needle pricks left little red bumps on his arms. Mark almost felt, when he thought about it, that it had been some sort of fantasy, some sick wet dream he had concocted up until he saw the pricks on his arm again and still felt a twinge of pain thinking about it.

Some sick dream that only his mind could come up with. And Madame Coudiva. . . what about her vision? Guess it didn't come true after all. He felt the bump on the back of the head from the bat. *Well, maybe only half true.*

That was enough for Mark. His traveling adventures were over. In the morning, it was straight to the airport for him. Mark lay in his bed a while waiting for the morning, watching as the sun came up through the shades in his room. He was restless, tired of traveling. Mark wanted to get back home, relax in his chair out by the pool.

That sounds good, he thought, turning over and finally letting himself drift back to sleep.

Three or four knocks on the door jolted him upright in his bed, Arthur's voice muffled.

"Mr. Malone, are you okay in there?" Mark laughed, it was a loud laugh, and almost maniacal except that Mark was barely awake when he did it. He called out, sliding his legs off the side of the bed and into a pair of Syracuse sweats he had gotten days ago.

"Yes, I'm fine. Just a minute. I'll be there in just a minute." He wiped the sleep out of his eyes and tried to straighten the bed head before he opened the door. No luck. He just opened the door. Arthur was there, a smile on his aged face, hat in his hands, towering over his sleepy client, the old man coming out in him.

"Come on, Mr. Malone, you ready to go or are you going to need more sleep?" Mark let him in without answering; let him begin collecting his bags and other assorted things. Arthur spoke up again.

"I can really understand why you might be tired, if you don't mind me saying?" Arthur waited for approval. Mark nodded his head. "She's pretty hot, Mr. Malone. But if that's not your type I could show you something a little bit different, maybe not as strenuous, but just as nice."

Mark looked up from tying his shoes.

What was Arthur talking about? Was Washington really this wild? I'm tying my fucking shoes. What makes Arthur think that I would want anything again? Mark finished tying his shoes and walked into the bathroom, packing the rest of his things into a small suitcase.

"What are you suggesting, Arthur?" Arthur didn't speak for a long time, not until he had finished packing all of Mark's things in the trunk and seated Mark in the back seat of the limo did he give a response. This made Mark a little uneasy about Arthur's plans. What did this old man know?

"It's called the Twist. It's a small place that another client of mine used to go to when he'd come to town. He loved it. He'd always come out with this big smile planted on his face. He'd keep that smile the whole time he was here. Believe me, it's good." The way Arthur said the last sentence was a little bit hairy.

*Believe **me**, it's good. Could this older man be getting the good stuff, too?* Arthur turned off the main street and drove onto the interstate, heading towards the airport. Mark leaned forward in his seat as Arthur described the things that went on in the club, using his hands through most of the detail, controlling the steering with his knee. Soon, he pulled the limo over in a parking lot nearby and shut the engine off.

"You know, you can always take a later flight. It's not the end of the world if you miss first class early in the morning. It's no different than first class in the afternoon. This is your last chance, Mark. Take it or leave it. I guarantee that frown will be turned upside down." Arthur made a frowning face and touched it with his two index fingers, turning it into a smile.

There must be some reason this keeps happening to me, Mark thought, rolling around the different experiences he had in his head from the last couples of days.

What if Arthur is just some weirdo that likes to maim and kill? But the description that Arthur had told him sounded reasonable. Arthur rolled up the privacy pad in between them and started up the engine. The limo continued in the direction of the airport.

So many things zoomed through Mark's mind.

What is this that's going on with me? I vow to never go on any adventures again and the following day one pops right up in my lap.

Maybe I can't get away. It just sounds so much like fate more than chance. He turned on the intercom.

"Arthur, I believe I'll take it." He could feel Arthur smile through the petition.

God, what was I getting himself into? The airport soon disappeared from view. *Here we go*, Mark thought.

The limo made its way out of the city limits, peeling around sharp and narrow streets, making its way to its intended destination. At least, Mark hoped that's where Arthur was going. It had been a long week for the man who sat in the back of the limo now. He could feel the energy practically ooze out of him and onto the seats. He was still a little bit drained from the other night, but the side effects of the drugs did little to stop his oncoming anxiety about where this old man was about to take him.

Thoughts and images filled his mind, making him remember all of those fun times he had with his roommates in college, taking trips to Florida and the northern part of California, far from his home in Beverly Hills. But now, his blood pumped through his veins even faster than it had with Missy, the young woman he had his first fling with. It was as if all things were finally coming to a close. His time for sewing wild oats had been over long ago, Mark agreed, but something about this trip made it seem like there was really an intended destination and he was actually on his way there.

The anxiety inside Mark soon ceased and he was a little calmer, less worked up. That was, until the limo stopped. The privacy pad lowered again and Arthur smiled up over it, tipping his hat to him.

"This is your stop, Mr. Malone. If you need anything, they know where to reach me; but I doubt that you will." Arthur got out of the limo and opened the door for Mark, watching Mark's expression as he stepped out into a new world.

It was an alleyway, a darkened corner of what only could be called the slums of Washington D.C. Mark had shivered when he got out of the limo at Madame Coudiva's house, but felt that he almost needed to have a heart attack here. Arthur saw the look on his face.

"Don't worry, Mark. You've made the right decision. Nothings going to happen, not unless you want it to." Mark glanced again at his surroundings.

It was midday in Washington D.C., but here it looked like nighttime. All of the buildings surrounded Mark, laying a dark overcast over everything, hiding the sun. Mark could see trashcans tipped over, a bum in the corner at the end of the alley, and even the old stereotypical scroungy cat that lingered in the dumpsters. It made its way around the limo, sniffing and looking; its eyes darting here and there, as if it heard noises from afar. Everything felt weird, strange, and almost dreamy, except for the door.

It was a door well below all the buildings, with several steps taking it down into what could only be a basement; the only door in the alleyway. And the place was quiet, too quiet, as if the world had stopped its intense ticking and just Mark, Arthur and the bum and his cat were there. But he saw indifference in Arthur's eyes.

"You know, looks are deceiving, Mr. Malone. Everyone knows that. 'You can't judge a book by its cover', they all say. And all of them are right. You can't, Mark. So don't try. Just go in. Let things happen."

And Arthur didn't have to point. Mark knew what he was talking about. Mark took a step forward towards the door, his hands fidgety and sweaty, almost like prom night, except he knew what was going to happen then. This, this was like closing your eyes and running, you don't know if there's something that can hurt you or help you. But, after running so long with your eyes open, Mark's mind was in tune with things that hurt and he knew how to avoid them. He took another step. Arthur stepped back, closer to the limo. Mark wondered what Arthur thought right now, wondered if he thought him a coward.

Oh, well. There's nothing Mark could really do about it. He was terrified, yet he still took a step, one after another, until finally he took his first step down onto the stairwell. That's when he stopped, turning back to Arthur.

My luggage, Mark thought. Arthur, again, was a little quicker.

"You're bags and things are safe here, with me. I'm going to ship them for you to the address listed on your business card, if you don't mind. You won't need them. Mark turned back to the door. To his surprise, it was opening. And behind it was a beauty. She was young, he knew, from the tenderness of her face, probably just turned 18, but her eyes held much more. Mark heard the limo start up and pull off behind him as he made his way down the steps, watching the young girl reach out her hand to him.

"My name is Jonna." He took her hand, wondering, in his mind, what would be the best etiquette for this place, for this young beauty, though the establishment was still unknown. Jonna had a soft, fair complexion and she was a petite girl, with long, dark black hair, yet her features were intensely soft. She had little make up on, just a little red lipstick that stood out on her face, among her other stunning features; blue eyes, small face, with curls hanging all the way around her forehead and temples, long eyelashes that blinked when she shut the door behind him.

The lighting was very dim inside, yet he could still see what she wore as she stepped in front of him. She had a black, skin-tight skirt on and matching black pantyhose, with no shoes or high heels on. She had long hair, yes, but it was up in a bun on the back of her head, long stringy pieces filtering down from the bun, making each feature of her face, neck, and neckline stand out even more in the darkly lit room.

As for the room, it was just an empty room, the walls an unidentifiable color with the amount of light given, probably a deep blue or green, a long hallway just over Jonna's shoulder. She looked at him now, in the dark, waiting for his eyes adjust. It was perfect in here, too. The air wasn't hot or cold, just perfect compared to the heat wave they had just left outside. Mark wiped the sweat from his brow with his hand. There was an eerie sense of silence between the two, until, after a few moments, Mark looked into her eyes.

"As you already know, this place is called the Twist." Her voice was soft, not ringy like most young girls her age, yet still youthful.

"You're name is Mark, is it?" She waited for an answer. Arthur mustn't have told her anything except his name prior to him coming here.

"Yes, it is." Jonna then reached out to Mark, her hands on his sides in moments, her face close to his. He could smell her red lipstick and the strange fragrance she had on her neck. Jonna's hands slid against his back and she pulled herself closer, her body pressing up on him.

She gently pressed her lips against his, her arms squeezing him closer. He wanted to touch her but held back, sensing, for some reason, that there was more than this. He looked over her shoulder and down the hallway. It was just as dimly lit as the room he was in now. He couldn't see more than a few feet. The kiss stopped moments later and she wiped the lipstick from his mouth with her fingers.

"Well, Mark. You're here. What is it you want to do? Do you want action or would you like to look around first?" He wanted to see what was beyond that hallway, what was down that corridor that made Arthur smile so much. Jonna was here for the taking, here, ready and more than willing for him to take his desires out on, but that feeling was in him, the feeling in the car he had, where he felt he was here for a reason.

"Jonna, I would really like to look around first." It was more of a statement than a request. His impatience was getting the best of him. She gently slipped her hands from around him and let her arms drop to her sides, taking his left hand in her right, walking him down the hallway. Mark soon saw doors appear, lining the walls after a few yards into the hallway, following the young Jonna deeper into the Twist. Jonna soon stopped in front of a door, releasing his hand so she could open it. She turned the knob.

Chapter 11

- NOT THE BEST OF IDEAS -

The plane landed in California with a rumble, jolting Nathan and Denise awake, along with other passengers in the first class seats, Nathan pulling himself up a little in the leather seat. Denise's hand was still deep in his pants. She recovered quickly when she noticed, averting her eyes away from him, her hand under the blanket pulling away from inside his jeans.

This can't be happening, she thought. *I need to get it together or I'll get caught*. She had been on many excursions away from home now and has never been photographed or caught on camera with another man. That would certainly ruin her image. And she wasn't about to have it ruined after coming this far.

She grabbed the napkin from under her drink on the tray in front of her and wiped off the juices that covered most of the top of her hand. Nathan scooted closer to her, breath penetrating through her shyness as he zipped up.

"You give a man no choice, do you, Mrs. Malone?" She scooted a little bit further away from him.

"You know I hate it when you call me that." He scooted closer to her, his hand exploring underneath the blanket as the plane slowed down on the runway, approaching the terminals at Los Angeles International Airport.

"I think married women are so sexy. You, Denise, make me dance on air when I'm inside of you. And that night at the club," Nathan squeezed her thigh, letting out a little moan in her ear, each finger tracing the slight outlines of her panty hose, the curve of her hips, everywhere that she wanted to be touched almost all at once.

He did have a way with words, she thought, looking deeply into his eyes for moments only, knowing that a little more and it would be too much.

Not to mention his strong hands, gradually feeling his grip loosen as the seatbelt sign blinked off from above, nearby passengers suddenly scurrying to get their bags from the above storage compartments.

Nathan stood up, adjusting his clothing so that it looked presentable; he sat the blanket in his seat and grabbed two casual zip suitcases from above. Denise sat in her seat, watching as the rest of the plane exited, still a little weak from Nathan's firm grasp.

Why was he here, she wondered for a moment, why he took the trip with her. He had never come back with her before. It had always been Paris nights and nothing else.

Then, it dawned on her.

This was an affair. He wanted more than just an on the side fling every year or so. Denise could tell by the smile on his face. He let the rest of the passengers by and then looked over at her, that same smile that captured her attention and many other pieces of her when they first met.

"So, how far do you live from here?"

Both Denise and Nathan made their way out of the plane and into hell, what they called the "rush hour" traffic within the several terminals. There were dozens of lines forming from the shops that lined the terminals, even more forming outside the restrooms; nowhere would there be a place of privacy. Echoes of flights, lost luggage, lost children, you name it, broke through what only could be called "Christmas-rush year-around" noise and played on the loudspeaker.

Denise was suddenly glad she had her bags shipped to her home right out of Paris's airport. Sure, it would take a couple of days, but it was worth it. The hassle in the Los Angeles airport would have been overwhelming. Denise prayed no one saw her here with Nathan. That would do real good for publicity. She slipped on her sunglasses from out of her handbag and made herself as unnoticeable as possible. She could feel, for some reason, every set of eyes watching her. It was really creepy doing something wrong in the public eye when it was in your town and it would be in the daily paper the next morning for everyone to see.

She took a deep breath and tried to relax. Nathan must have noticed this, too, rubbing his hand against Denise's secretly, trying, in some way, to comfort her as much as possible. She looked over at him through her shades. He was dressed in a pair of black slacks and a white polo shirt, his small, firm body holding a bag on each side. Even in a crowd of nobodies, he stood out. He smiled over at her at almost the exact moment she thought that. She turned back to the crowds of vacationers, trying as hard as possible to keep that wanting look out of her eyes. That's when the paparazzi nearly trampled her.

Instead of rushing into the terminals this time, the photographers made a line on both sides of the exit, waiting for her to exit with some new glamour shot or talk about her new and upcoming film. She really wasn't in the mood for this. With the leading man in the fight, her having to sleep with her boss to keep her part, this was not turning out to be a good week. And to top it off, her 'fling' decides to get a conscience.

But Nathan turned a bad thing around in a couple of seconds. Denise didn't have time to tell him anything. With a firm grip on his bags, he pushed them in front of him and made his way to the limo, leaving her behind to face the paparazzi. From the inside, Denise saw it all. Nathan handed his bags to the driver, motioning for him to place them in the trunk, then quickly, snatched the driver's hat and slapped in onto his head with one quick motion, tucking in his shirt as he walked back into the terminal.

The photographers didn't know what to think. There were no pictures taken; they didn't want to waste a shot on an "unknown" when they could get Denise Renfield-Malone. Within seconds, Nathan returned, empty-handed, her limo driver's hat on, holding his hands up to the camera lenses as he pulled her to safety inside the limo. He shut the door and made his way around to the front of the limo, her usual driver, a lost look still on his face, eventually got in on the passengers side after putting Nathan's bags in the trunk.

It was a true save. Nathan-1, Denise-o. She would never have had the imagination for that or the balls for that matter. But, as the privacy pad rolled down, Nathan flashed a victory smile and gave the driver back his hat, who was steaming but accepted it nonetheless, watching as this stranger, this imposter driver slide over the seat and into the back of the limo with the famous Denise Renfield-Malone. Who, in turn, was very, very grateful, closing the privacy pad even quicker than it had went down, her blouse slipping off onto the padded seats. Nathan-1, Denise-1.

*   *   *

It had been one of those days. Everything seemed to go wrong for Ms. Leonard. After leaving Mark's hotel room, her sister left her stranded at another hotel where all of the Syracuse football players stayed, stuck in a room with some thick-necked jock trying to finesse himself onto her. She bolted and made for the door at once. After that, she took a taxi back to her hotel.

It was the Capri Suites, a sort of generic Ritz-type hotel, complete with the little soaps, the online connection, and all the other blasé add-ons hoping that it will reel you in even longer. But she wasn't worried about staying and had already planned to leave that night back to Oregon when her phone rang.

Another wrong before the day had a chance to begin. It was six-thirty in the morning and she had just slipped her shoes off to get into bed when her father called her.

"Hello?" There was a silence before her father spoke.

"Hello, sweetie. How are you?" Cassandra exhaled deeply.

It was another one of father's trips, she knew it. Cassandra knew it was almost too good to be true. She was still off for another four days and she would have been able to relax for a couple of days at home, but apparently something was up with her father again.

"I know, I know. It's early and you're tired and all but I have something very important to ask of you, honey. I need you to help daddy if you can just for an afternoon. Can you do that for me, lamb chops?" Her father always called her pet names when he wanted something from her.

She remembered when she was just a little girl and wanted attention, when she would get in the way of daddy's line of sight with the old television he would say something like, "Honey bunches, could you go play in your room with your dollies? Thanks, sugar dumpling." She was about tired of those little names and wished sometimes that she had the guts to tell him to shove the names right up his ass but, alas, she had too much heart to do that. She loved her father and it seemed, sometimes, that he was the only one that really connected with her out of her entire family. And father's favors usually were pretty fun; she'd have to admit that. The last time was a little bit too fun but she could always handle herself well.

"Okay pops. What is it?" He was hesitating. It must be pretty important.

"I have a client coming in from Seattle and he likes entertainment. You know, the woman kind." He rushed himself through the next couple of sentences so she wouldn't think what it sounded like, which was beginning to sound like a call girl.

"And he needs an escort while he's here in D.C. and I'll be out of town and I need someone that is close to me that I can trust. He's a very private person but I told him the person I would get as my replacement is very adult and can handle any situations with the utmost confidentiality, if you know what I mean. I just need you to take him around town. He's a nice guy and this will close my 2 million dollar deal with him. If you can do this for me I would be most appreciative." Cassandra smiled.

So it was a sex fetish kind of thing that my father wanted to help him out with. Not a bit surprised. After mother left, it seemed apparent that father needed to find someone or something to occupy his "personal" time.

He knew all the best clubs and secret crevasses that were the "naughty" places now. He still was a loving old man, Cassandra couldn't deny that. He never really talked about things with her unless she wanted to know, which she really didn't. It almost kind of grossed her out thinking of her dad like that.

"Okay, dad. You don't need to say anymore. When do you need me there?" She was waiting for the answer. She knew what it would be even before he said it. He always put things off right until the last moment.

That's how he was and that's how he will always be. That's why mom was gone.

"I have a ticket reserved for you at the Syracuse airport, landing at the Dulles at 5:15 p.m., will that be enough time for you to get ready and rest up? Of course. What am I thinking? This is my little pumpkin I'm talking to. She's all grown up and lives in the real world now. Well, I have to be on the plane in an hour. There's a movie shoot there in a couple of days and I have to be there to oversee it. You know, I am the director and all."

For some reason, Cassandra knew he would throw that in there somewhere at the end of the conversation. He always had to state who he was and bask in the glory of being Harold Drindden, the great director. That's why Cassandra had changed her last name. She didn't want to have any fame from her father rubbing off onto her. She wanted to get the fame all herself if that's what she wanted. But she didn't want that kind of life, not at all.

She had changed her name to her mother's maiden name when he began to get famous.

He was good, yes, but it had taken him almost half of his life to get to where he was today. She smiled again and confirmed the times one last time before letting him go.

She had a couple of hours to sleep before she had to get ready and fly to Washington D.C. She had better take advantage of it. Cassandra unzipped the body suit from the back and slid it off, stepping out of it and towards the shower.

Might as well shower now, it will save more time, she thought. She turned on the hot water and let the steam fill up the bathroom, dipping one leg in at a time. Each foot dipped in gave her goose bumps all over her body.

Not unlike last night, she thought, remembering back to the handcuffs and body oils that Mark had gotten for them. She tried not to bring Alexis, Cassandra wanting it to be just her and Mark, but her sister caught up with her photographing after the game and tagged along. She was always a man stealer and had always been since their high school years.

Although Cassandra was older and more attractive, Alex had a fire built inside of her of some sort that just drove men to the brink of madness when they were with her. That's how it was with Mark last night.

Oh my god, he was great, she thought. It didn't take long for her to get turned on by him. Even at the airport she could sense something. She didn't know what, but something was there.

But, of course, Alex had to use her charm to manipulate poor Mark into doing so much more that it almost spoiled the night for Cassandra. Nevertheless, Cassandra knew that was just a phase for her sister and, hopefully, she would soon grow out of it.

But it's been a couple of years now and Alex had yet to grow up. Cassandra only wished that her sister had gotten a better job than just a cheerleader.

It was so demeaning, standing out there just clad in small outfits, dirty old men leering at you. Alex was raised better. But what could she do? Her sister was grown now and off on her own. She practically lived with the football team. It almost made Cassandra sick thinking about it.

So, instead, she thought about Mark again, her body tingling with delight at the thought of seeing him again. She had given him her address in Oregon but she really doubted that he would call her.

Probably married or something, she finally resolved, realizing that a man like that couldn't just be walking around without someone hanging onto him for dear life. But having a taste of something like that for Cassandra was always good; it showed that there was something out there that is at least worth her time. Most of the men she had gone out with were complete losers. Sports nuts, sex fiends, egomaniacs, greasy mechanic types and weirdoes seemed to fill her dating world like a plague. And if she did find any guy that was semi-decent, usually they were rich assholes that were stuck up their own asses or poor bums that leeched off of her as much as possible until she had to keep them at arm's length.

The bath water was suddenly getting a little bit on the cold side. Cassandra lifted herself out of the bathtub and reached for the towel above the toilet. She dried herself off.

Yes, Mark definitely had the ability to make me weak. She toweled herself down between her legs. She was still sore from last night. Cassandra pulled out a nightshirt and slipped into bed, letting herself drift off to sleep so she could get up in a couple of hours and start her repetitive life again in the morning.

Will anything ever change, she questioned, drifting off to sleep within moments.

Chapter 12

- AT A CROSSROADS -

Here is where the change began. Cassandra strode through the lobby of the Capri suites, travel bag in hand, biting her lip as if her life depended on it. She had just thought about what she had done by agreeing to her father's demands. She almost wanted to smack herself for saying yes. She was so exhausted last night she had forgotten what the last of daddy's "clients" had ended up getting her into. This one had had a sick fetish.

*   *   *

But it was with little girls in skirts. Cassandra couldn't forget the man's face when he was arrested for trying to pick up a little girl at a preschool down the street from where her father lived. Cassandra had gone out for some groceries and other things that morning and was on her way back to the house when she saw the man she was supposed to be taking care of getting pushed into the backseat of a patrol car. His name was Charles Finter. He was a local high-class corporate head, married with three children of his own, all girls. If that wasn't the sickest thing she had ever dealt with.

*   *   *

She almost wanted to call her father back and cancel but she was almost sure that he was already on his way to Paris for the movie that he was shooting.

At least he's not getting into trouble and doing something good with his time for a change, she thought, walking out onto the curb, looking for the nearest taxi.

Cassandra hailed a taxi and pushed her bags in the backseat with her, almost bursting from the tension in her head on the way to the airport.

Something is definitely going on inside of my head, she agreed, watching the world outside the taxi zip by, the airport in sight just ahead.

Something was happening out in the world, Cassandra thought, curling a lock of her hair around her finger, trying to rekindle some old nervous habit from childhood to release the tension she had inside.

She could feel the tension in the air, too, as she walked through the airport, retrieving her ticket on her way to the terminal. There was something definitely happening that she couldn't explain. It was as if everything was fitting together in some way, falling into place like a puzzle. However, she decided, she had to keep focused for this client of her dads, brushing off the feeling she had as mental stress caused by the last couple of days. Cassandra finally decided that she would just go there and enjoy her time off anyway, even though this wasn't really what she had in mind.

A book and a bath would be so much better, she thought to herself, watching as the rest of the passengers boarded, hands full of magazines, aspirin, candy bars, newspapers, whatever distracted them from the ground that they would be leaving behind moments after they boarded. She had her thoughts to do that for her. But, as she looked at the line of passengers bustling to get on the plane, she might need more than just her thoughts.

A drink wouldn't hurt either, she concluded, standing in line, a long line, filled from front to back with a myriad of people that she just did not want to be around right now. Sure, she was a people person.

But how much of people can you get before you've had your fill?

If her day couldn't get any worse, the passenger next to her had a screaming infant that constantly spit up, the flight was delayed while they waited in line for takeoff on the runway, and they were out of her favorite drink; Bloody Mary. She ordered two gin and tonics instead, devouring one then another, trying to drown out the noise that the infant passenger made next to her. It was hard to do so but, after her fourth drink, everything seemed to echo inside of her skull. The flight soon took off and, after a couple of minutes in the air, the infant was soon fast asleep. Cassandra had thought she would never get any peace and quiet, thought that she would never get time away from the noise of everything at once.

But something did take her mind off of the noise, off the wait, off the dry, foul-smelling air around her. It was the thought of Mark; a single thought, that crossed the path of her mind and sent her into another world. It was something he had done to her.

She still had a tingling from that night and that was strange. She had always considered herself strong when it came to men and her relationships with them. Of course, she was independent, yet she still carried herself like a woman, and wasn't scared of the masculinity that men gave off. It was a natural part of their ways; and that's what attracted Cassandra to Mark even more. It wasn't usual for her to linger on such escapades, which she knew was just that; an escapade.

Or was it?

It was definitely his fingers rubbing down the path of her spine when he was behind her that did her in. His hands were so gentle, yet so powerful. He had pushed himself in her from behind when Alexis had gone to shower the hot oils off. It was that look in his eyes. He stared her down, as if he had wanted a chance alone with her all along, only her, and had it now, showing her immediately his inner workings. She had come with Mark at the same time. He had brought a desire inside of her and it felt that this was only the beginning, their bodies sweaty and tired, when Alexis returned, her normal, fiery self ruining the moments after that.

But that moment, that single gaze that she had with his eyes almost disturbed Cassandra now, brushing away the small hairs on her forehead that escaped her hair tie earlier, feeling her body almost seep out that wanting feeling again, as she had done when Mark opened his door that night to let them in.

She needed to get in contact with him again, she knew, in the back of her mind, but how? He hadn't left her a number to call and she, this irresistible beauty, had left him a number that she didn't think he was going to call. But maybe he wasn't like the others she had met in the last couple of years. Maybe that's why she felt this way about him.

The plane soon landed with impatient passengers pushing out into the terminals to space themselves from the others and a very ill crew and captain, Cassandra heading for the baggage claim as quickly as possible. She found it at once and lifted her bags off of it, heading to the bulk of taxis waiting outside the skycap area. She hopped in one, the first she could get to.

It was another hour before she arrived at her father's house, the taxi pulling up on the massive five-bedroom home sitting back away from all the other bigger homes that sat on the streets. There were no cars parked out front so her father's guest must not have arrived yet.

Cassandra paid the fare to the taxi driver and slid out of the backseat, retrieving her two bags and a few bags full of things she had bought for herself while at the D.C. airport. The taxi pulled away and drove off, Cassandra digging in her pockets for the keys to the front door. Her father had given both of his daughter's keys to his homes just in case they were in town so they had a place to stay.

Cassandra's father had four homes presently, one in Maine, a condo in Florida overlooking the beach, and a loft in New York that he rented out during the winter and, of course, his main home, the one she stood before.

It was a beautiful home. The ceilings were low, which made each room look longer, and almost all of her father's walls in the home were covered with paintings that were the present decor that decade. She smiled when she thought of what Mark had said.

Paint for mostly rich assholes, she thought, dropping her bags in her room upstairs. Each room had a television and entertainment system. When father had bought this home, about seven years ago, he had the rooms completely gutted out and each one was given a bathroom. Originally, there were seven bedrooms, but as he added the bathrooms for each, two of the bedrooms just weren't able to be in the plans.

Cassandra's bedroom was simpler, less cluttered than all of the other bedrooms. She had taken out all of the paintings and left the walls barren. She liked it that way. It gave her room to think. Before she became a photojournalist, Cassandra had attended college at the University of South Carolina. It wasn't far from where her father lived and she could come home for a visit every-so-often. However, it wasn't long until her father had drawn the last straw; he had someone in his business that he wanted her to marry, waiting for his daughter to return for Christmas break. Of course, that was years ago. But Cassandra still had not too fond memories when she came here.

His name was Eric Sevantz. He was a stuffed shirt that filled her every second with loathing for the rich. She was well off and had no financial problems, that was true, but she didn't flaunt it like some others in the world. And he was one of those types; the stereotypical rich man with everything but a gorgeous gal by his side. He had majored in accounting, constantly relating his favorite jokes of how he liked being able to count his own money when he got older during dinner parties with her by his side.

And there were plenty of dinner parties to go to. Her father had premieres of his movies with all the rich and famous actors and actresses coming to his home to celebrate, Trump style. There was an assortment of drugs, men and women who catered to the needs of people at the party, and numerous other luxuries that only the rich could throw around to their guests. She was there, along with her sister, Alexis, dressed up for the occasion and smiling as hard as they could for all their father's guests.

She had been in college for four years then, majoring in journalism, with a minor in photography. It had been an easy major, but the stress of coming home to her father every holiday and at the end of each semester tore her apart. Eric Sevantz was there every time, drooling over her, constantly making his way into her plans while she was at home.

She didn't want that. Sure, he was an attractive man, with a nice frame and a nice smile, but he was more of a lap dog to her father than a person. And Cassandra couldn't deal with that.

Cassandra took off her clothes and slipped into some comfortable shorts and a matching t-shirt, making her way downstairs to see if there had been any messages on the answering machine. She grabbed a bottle of water out of the fridge and walked through the kitchen. It was completely stocked with enough food for an army and was as spotless as ever.

Even the ice trays were full, she noticed, looking in the freezer for a possible dinner tonight. *The butler was away, though,* Cassandra glancing at his work schedule on the kitchen note board.

He wouldn't be back for three more days, probably not even before then, she thought, knowing that her father didn't like anyone in the house except for her and Alex.

She clicked on the answering machine. There were three messages. One was from a producer in Paris, the other was a restaurant confirming a reservation for dinner a week from now for her father. The last message was a man's voice; it was the guy she was supposed to meet here. He stated that he was arriving late and apologized and that he would be there around two days from today.

He sounded charming, Cassandra thought, taking a sip of water and stopping the answering machine with her free hand.

Well, she thought, *there go my days off at home*. Cassandra would just have to find something to do until her daddy's guest arrived.

She really missed being at home lately. She missed the long, comfy sofas and the thick, plush pillows that filled her little apartment. Cassandra had spent months after the break-up getting her apartment just the way she wanted it.

In the last month, though, she had been traveling all over the states, covering different stories for her paper, always finding a hotel late in the night or early in the morning, constantly carrying with her a feeling of missing out on life. By the time she was finished with her projects in the locations she traveled, everything was closed and she couldn't tour the place. It felt like it wasn't even traveling.

That, she concluded, *was the only downfall of being a journalist*.

You didn't really have a lot of time for your life. You pretty much just went on another's schedule, the schedule of others' lives, using your time to fill theirs with what they considered to be something of value. But to Cassandra, her values had changed in the last couple of years.

*   *   *

It had all started with her last long relationship, Michael Harrison. He was tall, dark, and extremely handsome, sometimes too handsome, which she had found out all too quick. He was working as a photographer for a magazine called *Stylin*, a pretty fast-paced piece of work that kept him up late nights in his apartment. He had turned his bathroom into a dark room, hundreds of pictures scattering over the floor and on the walls. That's where Cassandra had taken a real interest in photography after college. She at least had Michael to thank for that.

Cassandra had taken a liking to him immediately. Both of them had lived in Oregon for a time and he lived down the hallway in the same apartment building when she was just starting out in her journalism career. In a couple of weeks, the long nights of coffee on the couch turned into long nights of passion in her bedroom.

It was a fast move for her, who had only been with very few partners and, from what he said, for him, as well. But those blue eyes held a past that Cassandra would eventually find out. Once Michael moved in, it wasn't too long before he began spending late nights out, coming back with a handful of pictures to show for his time.

But Cassandra knew that there was more to it than that. He was pulling away from her at night, sometimes staying up late at night in the bathroom, at his work, which seemed to consume him. He didn't eat most of the time and they had stopped going out at all anymore.

The time Michael had with Cassandra was slowly coming to a halt. One night, as he left the apartment for one of his late night excursions, Cassandra had decided to follow him.

She waited until he slipped out of bed and left, then she got in her car as well, following his red Lexus down through the streets and, finally, to a hotel room where Cassandra waited until it was safe to make her move.

You see, Cassandra was an innocent woman in comparison with the dirt that many others did. Sure, she had experimented with things like drugs and liquors, even strayed to the bi-sexual side once, which her sister does often without hesitation. But, deep down inside, she had always just wanted to be with one person for the rest of her life, without any surprises. It was just so hard for her to find someone like that. She knew the evil that people did, just didn't know that she would be caught up in it without knowing.

As she approached the hotel room door, she felt as though her life would change forever after this moment. Of course, she could've just been overreacting, but then again, what is life if you don't ever overreact sometimes? But she knew he wasn't photographing here and that it had to be some other woman.

Yes, he was handsome, she thought. *Many women want him.* But he moved in with me. *He loves me.* She played these things through her mind over and over as she built up the courage to reach her hand out to the door and knock. The knocks still echo in her mind to this day.

*　　　　*　　　　*

Now, her values were set, prioritized, actually working, whatever you might call it when life was functioning without problems. She might not have much of a social life, she knew that, compared to the other female workers that constantly had an assortment of men that they bragged about, but she was fine with that. Of course, that didn't mean that she didn't get any offers. Not even a day would go by when someone didn't come up to her on the streets or at work, or at one of her photo sessions and ask her out. But she had declined almost everyone, with the exception of Mark.

That brought Mark back to the forefront of her mind. She hadn't had time to really sit down and think about him in the last day or so. But should she? He was probably in some other state, making the best of the time he had, while she sat here, moping about. From what Mark had told her about himself and what she saw in his brown eyes, he seemed to have things together in his life. But, then again, that day she had met him at the airport, she knew he was married. He did that quick check to see if the ring was on his finger. And it wasn't. But if he didn't tell her, she didn't know. Maybe she was overreacting yet again. She had a tendency to do that.

Cassandra gathered up her thoughts and left the kitchen, shuffling her way through the house. It was really a beautiful home. She didn't grow up here but would have loved to. The house she had grown up in was long since torn down. It was years ago and she tried to forget the past, let it go, and let her mind chase after something that was tangible and here in the present. She needed to find Mark; at least find him so she would know if what she felt was real. She just needed a plan of action. She had two days before her father's client showed up here. Maybe she could find Mark by then. But where did she start?

*   *   *

Jonna led Mark into the room, which was dimly lit, but he could see shapes moving in the darkness in the corners of the room and, in the center of the room, there was a bed. Mark's eyes adjusted to the light and he could see that the shadows in the corners of the room were others like Jonna and him, a guide and a visitor, watching eagerly at the several on the bed. And there were several on the bed. The bed was enormous in size but was set lower to the ground, just barely two feet in height. There were four bodies on the bed, writhing in pleasure, two women and two men, naked and sweaty, panting in the stuffy room. One woman was on her hands and knees on the bed while a man pleased her from behind, and the other man and woman were in a sixty-nine position, mouths full of each other, pumping and groping at each other, constant moans out of stifled lips. Then the woman on top came. She was loud, out of breath, letting out syllables and cries that sounded like she was in pain, but her face said otherwise. It was covered in shadows but Mark couldn't mistake that look. She loved it.

Once she was done, she climbed off, taking a last look at the man that she had been with and then retrieved her clothes from the floor by the bed. She regrouped with her guide who took her from the room.

A woman from the corner of the room moved towards the bed, undressing quickly, her eyes on the stranger on the bed by himself. She climbed on the bed and he grabbed at her, Mark watching as she mounted him with ferocity, pounding away on him as she held onto the back of his neck, her face level with his. It wasn't long before he came. She was fast. The man pulled himself from her grip and seemed as though he was upset, gathering his clothes from the floor and rushing out of the room, his guide following after quietly. The woman on the bed looked at Mark. Jonna nudged him.

"She wants you on the bed with her. You can if you'd like to. Of course, there are other rooms with many different things in them. And, you can always have me at any moment, you know." Just then, the man on the bed pleasing the other woman came, his moans echoing in the small room and he soon departed as well, another man from out of the shadows replacing him. The two women were on him in moments, one sliding on top of his thighs, the other trapping his face in between her legs. All began to moan.

The bed in the room looked pleasing, Mark couldn't deny that. But something kept him at bay, even from the young Jonna, who was closer to him than before.

The sight of pleasure must be getting to her, he thought, looking into her eyes in the darkness. They were bright and full of ideas. Jonna shrugged her shoulders and made her way past the other guides and visitors in the corners, exiting another door that they hadn't come in through earlier, opening them up into a larger room filled with pillows and soft lights that made the room look brighter than the other, yet still casting shadows on everything. There were several couples here having sex, in different positions, mumbling and speaking to their partners as they moved, pleasure filling all of their faces by what light was shed on them.

Jonna turned to Mark.

"This one of my favorite rooms. I'll be right back, if you don't mind?" Mark waved his hand, stating that he was fine by himself for the moment. Jonna smiled and bounced away, into the pillows, approaching a man in one corner, by himself. The young girl slid up her skirt and sat down on top of the stranger, moving furiously on him, her hair coming undone from its bun on the back of her head, falling down her back, down to the pale round cheeks that bounced on the man's thighs furiously.

Mark couldn't stand this anymore. Something inside just told him that this was wrong. He had been with many women, yes, but not like this.

At least there was some decency in what I did, he told himself, watching as some of the visitors traded partners, even watching Jonna as she was swapped to another man. *Was this all it was?*

Was this the Twist? Mark had some weird things happen to him last night that he didn't approve of and, it seemed to him, that this was the exact same, all except for the drugs that they had given him. But this wasn't him. He didn't want this.

What he always wanted was the challenge, the excitement of the chase. This was just a brothel, a sex house that went unknown to the world outside. That's the way Mark would like to keep it.

Mark turned and found the door he had come out of and went through, passing the room with the single bed and through the previous door before that, walking back down the long hallway by himself. By the time he reached the door, Jonna had already caught up.

"Is there something wrong, Mark?" Mark turned to her one last time before he left. She was still out of breath from the last visitor that had her.

"Yeah, this is! All of this is. I have to go now!" Mark shut the door behind him, hailing the first taxi that he saw, making his way back to the airport.

Chapter 13

- "SAY CHEESE!" -

Something had happened. Denise lifted her head up from the back of the limo, watching as the security gates around her home came into view, pulling up into the massive paparazzi storm that seemed to rain down upon her. The limo pulled up to the front gates, the driver getting checked through the security booth.

"What's going on?" Nathan slid his pants on, looking out at the waves of cameramen and news vans that were parked at the gates.

"I have no clue!" Denise slid her skirt back down into place and straightened it with her hands, trying also to fix her hair in the small compact that she had pulled out of her purse.

What was going on was going to be taken care of pretty quick, Denise concluded, crossing her arms as they drove through security, looking out through the tinted windows as the paparazzi disappeared, replaced by the scenery of the landscape entering her home.

Denise had called the house several minutes ago at the airport and the butler had answered, stating that Mark had left days ago, going off on a couple of trips, he had told the butler, taking several bags with him.

So Mark wasn't there? Was there someone famous at our house?

Dammit, Denise thought, *security's not supposed to let anyone in that wasn't on the list; and there weren't many people on the list in the first place.*

Most of them were immediate family and that was only if they were scheduled to be arriving, and no one had done that.

And Mark wouldn't invite anyone over if he weren't here. Even he's not that stupid!

The limo wound its way around through the small garden they had at the front near the gates. The limo finally crossed over the wooden bridge up to the driveway, which could hold up to fifteen cars at a time, more if Denise let other in their six-car garage. But there was only one car parked in the parking area now. It was a red Jaguar, the model she had seen several times, since the beginning of her career and her and Mark's marriage. It was their lawyer. And their lawyer, Brent, was already in the house.

Yet again, as a reminder, Denise looked over at Nathan and almost winced in pain. *What was I doing?*

The limo driver held the door open as Denise and Nathan made their way out of the limo, the driver getting Nathan's bag and smiling at him.

It was more like a smirk, a little hidden grin that barely escaped his lips, Denise noted. Nathan ignored it but Denise wasn't about to. It was in her nature to tear at the weaker sex.

"What the fuck is so funny? You have something to say?" But the limo driver was prepared. He didn't take up a defensive position, just shook his head and reached into the front seat, pulling out a paper.

"No, Mrs. Malone. I just got the paper this morning and was trying to...." Denise didn't let him finish. She ripped the paper out of his hand and almost fell over when she looked at the front page. It was the Beverly Hills Commoner, a morning paper distributed to everyone in the Beverly Hills area. The headlines were in bold, as they always were; yet they seemed darker than ever, especially since her name was in them.

*   *   *

DENISE RENFIELD-MALONE CAUGHT IN THE ACT!

"Denise Renfield-Malone caught in the act?" Denise threw the paper at the lawyer, almost nailing him directly in the face with it.

"What the hell is this, Brent? I thought you were supposed to protect me from these kinds of things!"

Denise and Nathan were in her home now, far from the reach of the cameras or the smile that the limo driver had on his face before she fired him.

He wasn't smiling then, now was he?

Denise waited for her lawyer to say something. He didn't speak at all. In fact, he had the same smile on his face that the limo driver had.

"What? What is so fucking funny? Would you tell me please?"

Denise was about to burst. Nathan was by her side the whole time, waiting for a response from the lawyer also, still lost in the confusion of it all. He had thought that the paparazzi at her gates was normal. But, as he picked up the article and read it now, things dawned on him.

Someone had let out that they had pictures of Denise with another man besides her husband. Nathan could feel the pressure now as it sunk in. What was going to happen to him? His girlfriend was going to go ballistic!

The lawyer moved over to his briefcase on the kitchen counter and pressed the two tabs on the top of it together, both of them snapping open at once. He pulled a manila envelope out of it.

"Before I give these to you to see, I want you to sit your excited self down." He was cool, calm and collected, exactly what Denise had always known him to be. He was Denise's same age, probably just hitting his mid-thirties as well, and he smiled at her. He knew this temper of hers all too well.

She remembered when her and Mark had first met him. He was this calm and cool then. He had cost them a lot of money, that was a fact, but he had always saved them from any financial distress, which Denise always seemed to slip them into at the most inopportune times. She stopped her fussing, for the moment, and sat down.

"Okay. Now that you're a little calmer, I want to ask you a question. Your friend here might need to leave." Her lawyer looked over at Nathan, who was sitting down just now, hands clasped together, waiting.

"It's okay, Brent. He's my friend, he can stay." Brent nodded and handed the envelope over to Denise who, in turn, took a breath and unfastened the metal rings, sliding out the pictures.

"Do you have any secrets you don't want anyone to know about?"

It was her and Nathan, over two year ago, on the set of her third film she had done for Mr. Drindden. They were in his car, the top down, on the side of the road. She still had long hair then, before she had the makeover. The picture was a little blurry because it had apparently been taken in motion, probably someone driving by who snapped it at the last moment.

But who? She went to the next picture.

It was her and Nathan again, this time in her trailer, up against the wall. This one had been taken over a year ago, the last time they had seen each other before this last fling they had just returned from. She was still wearing her costume from the movie she was in, her face in mid-grunt, Nathan's nude form behind her. This made her a little uneasy in front of Brent. She looked up at him. His face was serious now. He looked over at Nathan and then back to her.

Denise saw Nathan, too, looking over the pictures himself, leaning over in his chair, his eyes not making contact with hers. Instead, they were focused on the next picture. It was her and a man she had almost forgotten about. It was another fling, at the man's home in Philadelphia. He was good-looking. His name was Benjamin Michaels.

It had only been just a few times, but the photographer looked like he had a time with this one, taking several shots, apparently following her throughout the week, capturing each time with Benjamin in at least five or six pictures each. Nathan leaned over to her and sighed, looking at her now, into her eyes.

"Who is that nice-looking guy?" Denise couldn't speak. All she could do was turn her head in shame, away from Nathan, away from Brent and the pictures, feeling the tears build up. All of this came so sudden.

Sure, they were flings, but these pictures did something that allegations could never do. These could ruin her as a person, not just as an actress.

Denise stood up, making her way to the window in the kitchen that overlooked all of the acres of land, all the way down to the gates and the paparazzi that flooded to get a glimpse past the gates.

"So that's what they're here for, huh? These fucking pictures! That's just great. Just great! Do they know, Brent? Do they know everything?" She turned to Brent, who had already dug into his briefcase again and extracted from it a thick pile of papers, handing them to her. She wiped her eyes and took them.

"They only person they know about right now is you, Nathan." Brent signaled over in Nathan's general direction. "You pretty much gave them identification they needed by being seen on the way from the airport. Nice stunt by the way, Nathan. That almost worked." His tone was a bit cynical, just enough to get across that what they had done he didn't approve of. Brent continued.

"All they have right now are allegations, some call stating that someone had some pictures, that's it. We don't know who it was that called. But I have a pretty good idea." Brent handed her the detectives' resume that Mark had sent him days prior, complete with a photo at the top right hand corner. He handed it to Denise.

"But the pictures," Brent cleared his throat, watching the two stiffen before him, "they came from Mark. He sent those to me. There wasn't a note or anything with it. But I really didn't need anything more, did I, Denise? That's when I had this typed up," motioning to the stack of papers Denise had in her hands. She stared at the resume hard, almost as if she were trying to burn a hole through it with her eyes.

"That piece of shit, no good fat ass! Emmett, you bastard! You fucking bastard! I thought we had a promise!" Denise was furious.

Everything was tumbling around her all at once. She had no defense. She was guilty in all aspects of the sense of the word. Denise balled the resume up in her hands and threw it across the room.

She knew what the paperwork was even before Brent had handed it to her. It was justice. She had betrayed Mark from the beginning and that poor schmuck, who had been the victim all along, or so she had thought, had finally gotten her back.

That prick! He had probably left here so there wouldn't be a scene. He was a smart one for doing that, she commended him, *because if he had been here, things wouldn't gotten way out of hand.*

Nathan stood up and rushed over to Denise, snatching the pictures out of her hands, his eyes darting over the rest of them.

He flipped to another picture. To his surprise, there was another man, and another. A total of four other men laid spread out before him in the photos in his hands.

"And who is this? And this? Holy shit, Denise, you've been awfully busy! Sure, I've been cheating on my girlfriend with you but, I'll be damned! I can't even beat your score! And to think I left to come here with you. Fuck you, you fucking tramp! This is what you get!" Nathan flared, tossing the pictures at her, the photos scattering all over the floor around her feet. She had never seen Nathan angry before. It was frightening. Denise stared down at the pictures on the floor and covered her face. Nathan left the kitchen then, Denise not bothering to follow.

There was no point.

This was too much for her to deal with all at once. Brent began picking up the pictures, listening as Nathan headed for the door and, once retrieving his bags, slammed the door behind him.

In moments, Denise glanced to see him walking down toward the road, not far from the little bridge down by the parking area. He was making his way toward the gates.

He would be devoured by the paparazzi. But maybe that's what he wanted, Denise thought, helping Brent pick up the pictures. Brent accepted the ones she had and slipped them into the manila envelope on the floor by Denise's chair. Denise sat back down while Brent put the folder back in his briefcase.

"So that's what movie stars do, is that it? You know, I remember a young woman that was nothing like that in those pictures. What happened?" Brent straightened his tie, loosening it a little bit at the same time. There was a small sheen of sweat over his brow as he waited for an answer.

"Brent, it's not like that. I ...Well I..." Denise was tired of it. "Well, I don't know what the fuck to say to you to make you feel better. There's nothing I can say to take back what happened in the past."

There. Denise had said it.

It wasn't a very good speech, but it would do.

However, Brent didn't seem satisfied with it.

"Oh, so that's it? The past. Is that what Nathan was? Doesn't look like it to me. What, was he getting ready to move in or what?"

"Fuck you, Brent! That's none of your business!"

"As your lawyer, I'm asking you and, when it comes to that, it **is** my business! This isn't about your past. It's about what you're doing now. It's about respect for other people and you seem to have none at all. Where's your decency, Denise? What about Mark? He probably went ape shit when he saw the pictures. I haven't received a call from him yet either; god only knows where he is."

That was the first time Denise had seen Brent angry since college. It made her smile.

Things were so much simpler then.

Oh, how I wish I was back there now. Brent unbuttoned the top button of his shirt and then the cuffs at his wrists, loosening the tie more and slipping it over his head and into his briefcase with the pictures. He was red in the face as he looked at her, shaking his head, almost as if he were her father.

"You have any water? It's fucking hot in here!" Denise nodded and pointed to the fridge where they kept the bottled water. Brent took two from inside the fridge and handed her one, swallowing a few gulps of his own as she opened hers.

"I really don't know what to do, Denise. You know that, don't you? I don't understand why he didn't just sell you to the newspapers right then. He should have. That's how it is out there in the world, right? Showbiz?"

"What do you think, Brent? It's a dog eat dog world out there. Most actresses are worse than me. They'd kill for some of the parts that I've had. Of course, everyone's my enemy when it comes down to it. That's how Hollywood is. It's all a competition. But you wouldn't know about it, now would you?" Denise doubted that he ever would.

"What, you think I don't struggle in a competition with other lawyers? Sure, I've got you as a client but that isn't enough. I've got four other movie stars and they're all addicted to crack or some other fancy drug that's been invented to make you look like a moron to the press. They're pieces of shit wrapped up nicely, that's all. Shit, Denise, you're not the only one who's got problems!"

That was true, Denise thought, sipping at her water. *But why worry about someone else's problems when you've got plenty of your own?* That reminded her. She had to do something about Nathan.

"Brent, could you get Nathan a taxi to take him to the airport? He'll get eaten up by the paparazzi. He's never seen anything like that and he wouldn't be able to handle it. I'll read through the paperwork and we can talk when you get back, okay?"

Brent nodded in agreement. "We'll continue this later. But, when you read that, just remember, that's the best deal that you're going to get with a case like yours."

Brent gave her a weak smile and began to leave. He patted her on the shoulder as he left, Denise listening to his car start up a few moments later outside, leaving to catch up to Nathan.

Brent was mad, too. She could tell by the way he had looked at Nathan. Maybe it wasn't so good of an idea to have hired an old flame to be her lawyer after all.

At the time, it had been harmless because she was married, after all. But, now that she thought of it, it had definitely been a mistake.

They had been through so much together. Now, it seemed to her that she just pulled people into her problems with her.

Brent had always regretted not marrying her and going to law school instead. But that was the life he chose and he understood the consequences. It wasn't until he became her and Mark's lawyer that he finally told her how he felt. Brent had even forgiven Denise for Mark, stating that he was just a rebound lover gone too far. But Denise saw it all disappear in his eyes when Brent saw Nathan.

Probably before that, she thought to herself, her mind going back to the envelope that held all those pictures.

Denise hefted the divorce papers in her hand and crossed her legs, sitting them down in her lap. She began to read what the rest of her life held. It didn't look very promising.

Chapter 14

- AN IMPROMPTU ENDING -

Cassandra had finally found a way to locate Mark. She had found the limo company that had dropped him off. The driver gave her Mark's flight schedule and, after a little coaxing over the phone, found out that Mark was scheduled for departure from the Dulles airport, where she had just arrived at, of all places. She couldn't believe it at first.

"Are you sure he's here in D.C.?" The limo driver almost seemed hesitant to acknowledge his own reading from the printed itinerary in front of him, hearing the desperation in Cassandra's voice.

"Yes, ma'am. He's scheduled for departure at 4:30 p.m., a direct flight to the Los Angeles Airport. His bags have already been checked and I dropped him off early to wait for the flight, Ms. Leonard."

Cassandra thanked him and clicked her cell phone off, racing upstairs to her luggage. She changed quickly, taking a passing look at the clock by her bed.

2:50. It would take me an hour to get there from here and, with parking, I would probably make it in time just before the flight left.

She slipped on a pair of jeans and a gray form-fitting t-shirt she had in the bottom of her bags that she had bought in Syracuse a few days earlier. Cassandra grabbed her purse and shoes and made her way for the garage.

What was I going to say when I see him? Hi, Mark, I was just hanging around in the airport and saw you, so I thought I would come by and say hello? No, that was ridiculous. She just needed to tell him the truth.

But what was the truth?

Could I just open up to him and expect him to understand? No, it couldn't be that easy. Cassandra opened the garage door, flipping the lights on with the switch by the door.

Her father had three cars that he let his two girls use. One of them was a Ford Expedition. He traded it in every year on a newer model, keeping the color the same; a forest green that constantly reminded Cassandra of the wilderness. The other two vehicles were cherry red; her father's favorite color, and both of them had sheets draped over them. She slid one sheet off. It was his favorite; the 1937 Cord 812. There weren't too many around anymore and her father had always told them to be careful when driving it. She slid the other sheet off, the 65 Mustang shining out at her.

He had four other cars parked at the far end of the garage, covered in drapes as well that he didn't let anyone touch. Those were his pride and joy.

Cassandra opened the door to the Mustang and slid in the seat, reaching for the keys in the glove compartment. She turned on the engine and pressed the automatic garage door opener that was in the car. The garage door hummed to life and began to rise. Cassandra backed the Mustang out of the garage.

Mark paid the taxi driver and got out of the car, watching as it drove away from the airport. It was already 5:30 p.m. and he had missed his flight.

Arthur had really driven me way out of the way to that club, he thought to himself. He hadn't noticed until he had to make the drive back to the airport.

The Twist. Mark was disgusted now. It hadn't really hit him until he was standing there, watching all the others. It hit him all at once. The past week of his life had turned into what he was standing there looking at now. He almost wanted to crawl inside a hole and never come out. He didn't necessarily regret the things he had done because he had enjoyed them all.

Of course, he enjoyed them all differently than the rest. But he did regret what happened with Jessica now that he thought about it.

I shouldn't have even gone into her house. I knew what she was doing by inviting him over. Well, he didn't know the final outcome, which still made him ache inside a little bit when thinking about it. And the Twist just seemed like a recreation of that night full of mistakes.

Mark pushed through the crowded Dulles airport terminal and to the check-in booths that lined the entranceway as soon as he walked in. He made his way to the airline that he always used and pulled out his i.d., waiting for them to enter it into the computer.

I really don't want to have to go home now. He knew that the divorce paperwork had already been sent to Denise. He had called Brent when he stopped for something to eat earlier after missing his flight. Brent had told him that Denise had just gotten in from Paris when Brent had arrived.

And she had even brought one of her flings with her. That was ridiculous! But Brent said she signed the paperwork before he left. It was over and done.

Mark could start over again without having to worry about getting back on his feet. He had gotten half of everything. Mark smiled at that, thanking the clerk for changing his flight to the next one and turned around, almost running into Cassandra, who stood now, face to face with him. She smiled at him. She was even more beautiful than before.

"Hey. Remember me? I heard you were here so I wanted to come see you off." She reached out and gave him a huge hug. She lingered with the hug a moment then let go, coming back to his side where she had been.

"Could you go for some coffee before your flight?" Mark nodded his head, still amazed that she was there.

"I didn't think I'd see you again." Mark reached out and gave her a hug this time, folding up his ticket into his back pocket.

Cassandra relayed her story of the last couple of nights since their encounter that night and apologized for how her sister had acted. Mark could see that she really meant it. He couldn't help but ask her.

"Was it just me or did you not seem too enthused about your sister being there? Don't get me wrong, I enjoyed it, but I was just expecting you. It sort of took me by surprise that there was someone else."

"I hope you don't think I'm terrible. My sister gets a little crazy sometimes. That wasn't me, believe me. Well, at least some of it wasn't me." Mark sipped at his coffee.

"Well, what part of that night was you then?" It took Cassandra a couple of seconds to answer. Cassandra dipped her tea bag into the cup and let the hot water soak into it, spinning it around with a coffee stirrer.

She was really thinking on this one, Mark noticed.

"Okay, you got me. I can't hold out any longer. Mark, I came here to see if you felt anything for me. You know, more than just that. I don't know what came over me but, that day we met, I couldn't help but talk to you. I don't know what it was. It felt like I had to."

"Like a calling?"

"Yeah, you could say that. I never really believed in things like that, though; well, not until recently." Mark understood her completely. He had never believed in it, either. At least, not until last week, which seemed to leave an impression on him like he had never had before.

Cassandra looked at him, this time with intense interest, pulling a newspaper out of her purse. She handed it to him.

"I bought this at a news stand here. I was waiting for you so I started browsing when the title caught my eye. Once I read it, I couldn't believe it. What's going on, Mark?" Mark looked at the heading, which was what caught his eye when she handed it to him.

"'TEMPTRESS CAUGHT IN SEX SCANDAL!!!' Interesting title. I wouldn't go that far. They are quick, aren't they; don't waste any time? Well, now you know, don't you?"

"Yeah, I guess I do. What happened exactly?" She leaned closer. Mark sipped at the last of his coffee as he skimmed through the article, noticing that they had "added" information, exaggerating a little more than the situation really was, which was normal for the tabloids.

"I had some pictures given to me a few days ago by a friend that gave me the ability to wave goodbye to the marriage altogether. Yeah, you could say she was in a sex scandal. But I have no idea how this got out though, unless my lawyer released some information. But he usually doesn't do anything without my consent, or at least, he never did anything before. The divorce will be final in a couple of days. The paperwork's already been signed. All I have to do is move my studio out of the house. But I thought I'd stay away for a couple of days just to let it cool down, you know." Mark didn't know what else to say. He didn't know much himself.

He didn't know what Denise was going to do now that her career was ruined.

Maybe she could work as a newspaper add model or something, Mark joked, trying to hold back from gleaming with happiness.

That's what Denise deserved. She had been so shitty to everyone the last couple of years; she needed to be taught a lesson. It wasn't that he didn't love her, which he did. She just needed a new outlook on life. *And boy, was she about to get it.*

"So, what are you going to do now that you're divorced? Go on some crazy sex spree with as many women as you can or something?" Mark laughed to himself, trying to conceal the truth in his face. Cassandra laughed at him, at the same time pulling her hair up with a tie to hold it up behind her head. She paused when Mark was caught staring at her. He got back to the question.

"I wouldn't go that far. Really, I don't know. I've started getting ideas for some new paintings, if that's what you mean. I was thinking of taking that up again, just to see if I still got it."

"Actually, that's not what I was talking about, but it's good that you're starting what you like to do again. What I was talking about was are you going to jump right back into the dating scene again or what?"

In all the years that Mark had been alive, which really wasn't that many when it came down to it, he had never met a woman like Cassandra. She was straight forward, truthful, seemed to take in everything he said with the most heart-felt consideration. What was happening between them?

Cassandra could sense that he was asking the same things that she had been asking herself on the car ride over here. She needed to bridge the gap between them and quick, before Mark decided that he needed time to think.

"Mark, I'm not asking you for anything serious, at least, not right now. I just feel something between us and want to see if it will work. Would you be up to that? I know this is out of the blue and everything but, my father is out of town for the next couple of days and I have the house all to myself. I would love for you to come and stay with me and give me some much needed company. We could eve maybe make some sense of this madness. Sound good? Oh, please say yes!"

Mark stood up and took both finished cups and threw them in the trash. He turned to her.

Man, was this a week or what? So many things have changed, gone awry, yet things managed to fall into place. The idea made him smile. And, to top it off, Cassandra, a stranger that he barely knew, took a liking to him. Mark was almost at a loss for words. But that wouldn't do here, not now anyway. He needed to say something. And he wasn't about to say no.

"That sounds great, Cassandra. Is that what you want me to do, go with you?" Cassandra lifted herself off the chair in the coffeehouse and looked around the airport. It was still busy at

Dulles. Of course, it was constantly busy. People were going to and fro, here, there, almost everywhere at once, yet the time between Cassandra and Mark seemed to slow down. Cassandra looked at this man, Mark, a newly divorced man, an artist, an intense lover; someone that she had been attracted to since their first meeting.

"Yes, I do want you to stay, Mark. At least spend some time here with me and see if there's something more. I would love for you to stay. That's why I'm here right now."

Mark took her hand in his, pulling her closer to him. Mark could feel Cassandra's breath waver when he was close, saw her eyes grow weak inside their emerald depths. He kissed her.   Time slowed even more. Mark could feel his senses come alive with thoughts of them being together. If he didn't take this time with her, it might not ever happen again. He smiled an old smile when they stopped kissing.

"I guess I'll take that as a yes." Cassandra pulled the car keys out of her pocket and slid her purse over her shoulder, leading Mark to the car outside the airport.

Being divorced might not be so bad, Mark thought to himself, staring over at Cassandra in the driver's seat. He could see it now. He had his whole life ahead of him again. He didn't want to make a mistake like he did last time with Denise. That was definitely a mistake. He had to admit it.

At first, it was two kids living it up with riches in a fantasy world but now, as Mark grew older, he knew that there had to be some sense of security and foundation in order for a relationship to work. Of course, with the past week as a basis for him starting over, that didn't go to well but, then again, it's always good to start off with a bang. And Mark knew that he had done just that.....and then some.

Hell, I could probably even write a book about my experiences this week. But what would I call it?

The idea of a title flew from his mind as Cassandra tapped her foot on the gas, the Mustang zooming down the city streets, past the landscapes of Washington, D.C., into some future that was still not yet known, still waiting to be.

Maybe things would work with Cassandra. Maybe I would become the painter I used to be, I didn't really know right now. All these questions made their way through his mind, digging and probing, asking without answering. The world was, indeed, a place filled with questions.

But Mark was in no rush to find out just yet.

The End

AUTHOR'S NOTES

The moment I wanted to publish this book series was the moment that I found out that Isaac Asimov was a pervert. From that moment on, I knew I wanted to write erotic fiction. Many of the great writers that I have read stuck to one genre. They are also great men/women in their own right. But Asimov had balls. Thanks Isaac!

About the Author

Little is known about the author, TITUS STRONG. Taking his name from a classic Shakespearean dramatic hero, the author writes stories that fill the imagination with lust and humor, all the while waiting for his own next sexual conquest, forever filling his time with fantasies that wait to be fulfilled themselves.

Coming Soon From TITUS STRONG:

- ♥ How Santa Ate My Cookies and other Festive Tales of Erotic Fiction
- ♥ A Corporate Feeling: Book Two of a Man's Romance Novel